Rubdown
by
Jon D'Amore

Based on a story by
Jon D'Amore & Laura Fuino

ADVICE & LEGAL STUFF

Rubdown ISBN: 978-0-9853000-9-8

Jon D'Amore and his writings are represented by Howard Frumes of the law firm Alexander, Lawrence, Frumes & Labowitz LLP.

Cover design and graphics by JT Lindroos (www.jtlindroos.carbonmade. com) based on an original idea by Irene LoPresto (www.reflexgraphix. com). Sunset photo by Jon D'Amore.

Print layout and formatting by Steven W. Booth, Genius Book Services – www.GeniusBookServices.com

Back cover photo by A. Friend

Published by JGD
Printed in the USA
Rubdown – First Edition

TABLE OF CONTENTS

DEDICATION

To those in my life
who've made my writing and my happiness possible...
It's been a slice!

John Lennon

October 9, 1940
to
December 8, 1980

"Was she told when she was young that pain would lead to pleasure?"

vi

ACKNOWLEDGEMENTS

To repeat myself from my last book, one of the reasons I continue to write my stories is because people around the globe have told me I succeeded in my goal…which has always been to bring pleasure, entertainment and a smile to the world. That's why I take these narratives within me and bring them to life. The fact that people continue to enjoy what I do is a rush not many can fathom. As far as that other codicil mentioned on the Acknowledgements pages of The Boss *Always* Sits In The Back, Deadfellas, The Delivery Man and As Long As I Have Lips about wanting a comfortable, relaxing life for myself…let me reference a quote from The Delivery Man: "It's always when you think everything's going your way that life comes around and gives you an enema." For now (because this too shall pass), I can say with validity, fortitude and conviction that truer words were never written or spoken.

Thank you to all who've enjoyed my stories…and I hope you'll continue to do so.

The happiness in my life has always been due to my parents, Ann and Carmine 'Rocky' D'Amore. I love them and they will always be in my heart.

Thanks to: Eileen Saunders…for saving my life; Stuart Aion; Jennifer Duke Anstey; Carmine Appice; Glorie Austern; Steven & Leya Booth; Cameron Burke; Lee Chiacos & Donna Massello-Chiacos, Michael D'Amore; Tom & Doris DeFranco; Debra Denker;

Chantel Figueroa; Peter Flora, Laura Fuino, Gail 'GB' Geoia; George & Eileen Herberger; Ray Koonce; JT Lindroos; Irene "Rene" LoPresto; Mitch Levin & Donna Mazzola; Stan Morrill; Robert Peters; Julia Peterson; Les Reasonover; Louise Rittberg; Carol Ross; Chris & Nancy Swift; Lisa Tracy; Monty VanderMay; Betsy Walker; Ed Wright; David & America Young…all believers in the dream, in addition to being caring friends and relatives.

The remaining space on this page is for "industry people" who wholeheartedly deserve some ink: Diane Lombardi-Fleming, connected since birth (our parents were best friends), for her creative support and insights, and for inspiring me to bring each and every highpoint of my creativity to an even higher level. Most importantly and sincerely, Howard Frumes, my legal representative and a dedicated believer who stood by my side knowing it would finally happen. He's truly one of the good ones. Trust me on that.

FOREWORD

I like to refer to Rubdown as, "A woman's Shawshank Redemption with an erotic twist."

Jon D'Amore and I met by chance several years ago at a printing shop in North Hollywood while we were each having scripts run off. I noticed his name on a newly printed copy of The Boss *Always Sits In The Back* and began speaking to him in Italian, a language in which I'm fluent. But all he could do was reply with a smile and a pleasant, "I'm sorry, but no capisi."

As we discussed our screenplays, I told him about a story I had started writing but was stuck and unable to move forward with it. He gave me a copy of The Boss to take home and look over. It didn't take long for me to clearly see his talent. A few days later I asked if he would be willing to collaborate on Rubdown and he agreed…but only if I stuck to a rigid writing schedule, as he was in the midst of a couple of other projects.

And that's exactly what we did.

We would meet, sit on his deck overlooking the San Fernando Valley or by his pool…one of the many benefits of living in Los Angeles…and write.

The story quickly took form.

Needless to say, writing with Jon was an adventure and a learning experience. You know when they say, "It's not about the destination, it's about the journey"? Well, that's *exactly* how it was.

We immersed ourselves in research and treaded into known and unknown territories. We watched countless films with twists and intricate relationships. We also attended a few "special parties" to know the details of what went on at them, the people who attended them, the conversations that took place and the hedonistic enjoyment that could be experienced when stepping away from the mores of mainstream society.

Once the screenplay's first draft was completed, we had a table reading with wonderfully talented and well-known actors, most being close friends of Jon's. After a few more readings, with each one helping us find ways to improve the story...the script was ready.

Meeting with producers who claimed interest in the screenplay is a movie in itself. One told us, "I *love* the story, but take the rubdowns out!" Jon and I looked at each other in disbelief, laughed and sardonically asked, "Then why would it be called Rubdown?" We offered to write a new script for a fee, but like most "so-called Hollywood producers" who are happy to tell writers what to do, when the topic of "money" is brought up...their excuses are often more fictional and fantastic than the scripts they're telling you to write (or re-write).

That collaboration was never brought to fruition, and we were happy to have walked away from it.

We stuck to our vision. Not only did we have a unique, erotic, intriguing and heartwarming story, but when all is said-and-done, there's a lifelong friendship between Jon and me to show for it.

Having already written and published four books, The Boss *Always* Sits In The Back, Deadfellas, The Delivery Man and As Long As I Have Lips, I know Jon has a few more he plans to complete in the future, but he was inspired to take our script for Rubdown, add much more detail, filled in the backstories of the heroine and individual characters that couldn't be expressed in the mandatory 'limited page count' and confines of a script...and turned it into this book now within your possession.

Jon loves what he does, and I'm grateful that he puts so much passion and dedication into his work. I'm *also* grateful that after so many years, we still call each other "dear friends."

Laura Fuino
North Hollywood
2020

PREFACE

Lost and confused.

That's where I was during the writing of this book. It was one of those unexpected events that happen in your life by someone you'd never believe was capable of doing such a thing. Someone who promised they'd *never* do such a thing. People have pointed out that what took place came right out of my third tome, The Delivery Man, and that I had unwittingly handed the playbook to the other team.

True friends from New Jersey, Virginia, Colorado, California, and most of all, and most unexpectedly...New Mexico, where I had spent the last six years of my life, chose to make sure I survived.

Having lived my first 46 years within a mere 15 minute car ride to midtown Manhattan and 75 miles to the Atlantic Ocean along the New Jersey shoreline, and then for 14 years it was another short drive to Hollywood's Sunset Blvd and 25 miles (on the nose) to my favorite beach in Malibu, I then relocated to the *very* quiet town of Santa Fe, with its nearest ocean 825 miles away (trust me on the mileage. I've driven it several times just to see the Pacific). It was like taking a fish out of water and putting him in a place that didn't know how to handle, nor favor, fish like him.

But I did it for the happiness of another...because that's what you do sometimes.

As the story within Rubdown shows...not all who portray themselves to be friends, even the closest ones...truly are. Often, they don't show their inner and true dark side for years, sometimes decades. And you never discover that…until it's too late. *Way* too late.

Because that's what happens sometimes, too.

To put it bluntly, had it not been for those who stepped up to 'be there' for me, this book would not have been completed, nor would it be as good as it is (well, at least *I* think so), and I wanted to recognize them in the Preface so they know how important they were and are to me. It's amazing how reality imitates art…which imitates reality. That's what makes life such a slice.

Since we're on the topic of friends who've been there through the "thick and thin" of life's travails, I'd be remiss not to mention Laura Fuino, the woman who brought me the beginnings of a story that would evolve into Rubdown, along with the fun and hedonistic pleasures it brought during my 14 years in Los Angeles. As noted in this book's Foreword, Laura perfectly recalled our initial introduction to one another, how hard we worked to bring Rubdown's story to fruition, and by recalling just one of the *many* "meetings" with producers and pseudo-producers from L.A. to Europe.

But my recollection goes a little beyond what Laura conveyed, so I'll relay *my* version of Rubdown's genesis.

After Laura and I met in that North Hollywood printing shop, after she read my screenplay for The Boss *Always* Sits In The Back, and after she asked me to co-write a story she had written only 22 pages of, I was honest in stating that I was in the middle of a screenplay project I was committed to finishing. At that time, co-writing scripts was an offer I was somewhat-regularly being asked to do as I had just completed a few well-publicized, successful table readings of the screenplays for The Boss, The Delivery Man (each cast with well-known TV and film actors) and For What It's Worth, a 'short' script I had received a local award for. I believed I would find Laura's pages unreadable or poorly constructed, and was sure it wouldn't be formatted into the mandatory screenwriting style used at that time. Working on *another* script, and with a novice no-less, wasn't something I was looking to do at that moment. Not wanting to hurt her feelings, and since we shared an "Italian connection," I suggested she send me the nearly two dozen pages she had written. I was sure I would read several pages, then put it aside.

But everything that I had assumed would turn me off of the project…I found I was mistaken. Laura's well-written pages proved to be the beginnings of a story that literally touched me, and I wanted to see it completed.

I then took her invitation to co-write the script to the next level.

I gave Laura a list of my "requirements" that I expected writers to live up to if they wanted to partner with me…a list that usually turned them away or caused them to falter and break the deal.

Knowing she was a single mother attending a local college, in addition to working on her acting, writing and singing career, she was also scheduled to travel to Europe at least twice over the next several months, I told her each of us would be responsible for the completion of certain sections of the story on a strictly adhered to and timely basis, and she would need to dedicate at least one six hour session per week to meet with me to go over the pages we had written the week before.

Even during her trips to Europe, Laura was on the money with each of my demands.

I also told her that *I* would have the final say and would be the one to meld the separately written sections into the cohesive story Rubdown would become. This was usually the dealbreaker for most writers.

Laura agreed and had become a pleasure to work with.

At some point it was determined that a little "research" into the L.A. swinger and private club scene needed to be done, and though Laura had a strict sense of Italian morals, seeing as it was advantageous toward the facts within our story, she agreed.

It wasn't hard to find such locations and gatherings in L.A., and we voyeuristically detailed what needed to be documented. Though my years in the music business brought me to many similar parties, it was a first for Laura, but what it brought to the story was invaluable.

The woman I agreed to write Rubdown with had proven to be a dedicated trooper for the cause and to the benefit of our goal... and it has *always* been an honor to call Laura Fuino my co-writer of Rubdown's screenplay, a partner in the business of promoting it, and a true friend.

The names in this story have been made up, or they've been taken randomly from my phonebook...and they're not intended to be, in any way, conducive to the characters they may portray in this fictional story.

I use *italics* and ellipses (such as: ...). Why? Because that's the way we speak! They are there to alter the way you read.

Italics *emphasize* the specific word.

Ellipses are used as a timing rest...while staying on the same subject.

The italics and ellipses make reading this story more enjoyable and brings the characters to life.

As usual, I've included a Cast of Characters (in order of their appearance) at the end...just in case you need to reference it from time-to-time.

Oh, and if the last six paragraphs you've just read sound familiar...you may want to check out The Boss *Always* Sits In The Back, Deadfellas, The Delivery Man and As Long As I Have Lips.

Enjoy!

CHAPTER 1
Jessica's Dream

Brentwood is one of those well-to-do Los Angeles communities that tourists and commuters pass through as they travel east along Sunset Blvd on their way from the Pacific Ocean to Westwood, Bel Air, Beverly Hills or Hollywood. The hamlet's most prominent and least favorite memories are the two 1994 murders on Bundy Drive, and the final Rockingham Estate destination of a sixty-mile slow-speed car chase by police and news choppers that resulted in the historic O.J. Simpson trial. Those remembering back even further recall Marilyn Monroe's August 3rd, 1962 alleged suicide in her cul-de-sac home on 5th Helena Drive.

But at 9:30PM on Thursday, May 8th, 2014, while dining in Valentina's on San Vicente Blvd, no one had a reason to ponder such things.

Comfortably seated at tables and booths, patrons relished appetizers, entrees and desserts, consumed drinks, spoke in soft tones…and listened to the pianist, Jessica Farber.

Valentina's was the 31-year-old musician's second home every Thursday through Sunday evening.

Entering the front door and approaching the podium, guests, both regulars and first timers, would be greeted with a smile by Charlie, the classy 67-year-old manager and maître d', and then dine on gourmet fare overseen by Constance, the head chef.

This particular evening was Jessica's fourth anniversary at Valentina's, and though elated to have been there that long, no one could tell because every time she performed, she did so with full enthusiasm.

Playing the piano for an audience, *any* audience, always brought her joy. *Always.* It was all she ever wanted to do. Once her fingers touched the keyboard, the talent Jessica had honed as a child and throughout her life effortlessly flowed through them… and prominently on the fourth finger of her left-hand was her wedding ring.

The only thing that brought Jessica more joy than performing was her marriage of six years to Leon Farber, a handsome, '*meant for the big city*' Potter Township, Pennsylvania boy who was smart enough to leave the middle-of-nowhere, move to L.A. and get a degree from UCLA. That was where the two of them met. He became a successful graphic designer and Jessica was *very* proud of him.

At five-foot-seven, with stylishly short auburn-hair and a body she was too shy to expose, Jessica would never be mistaken as "a stunner." Those who knew her described what she had as a "natural, inner beauty," though Leon often referred to his wife as "plain."

It bothered her that he felt that way. It bothered her more when he would say it.

Jessica knew she couldn't compete with the *average* beauties who converged daily from around the world into the 503 square miles that is Los Angeles.

Nor did she care to try.

"The hopefuls," as they were known, disembarked daily from planes, trains, buses and cars, each dreaming of attaining a career in film, modeling or TV. Others came to attain a successful partner of either sex…and to share in their lives and fortunes.

There was also an equal number of "the hopefuls" who departed the same way and in the same frequency, but with their dreams and desires unfulfilled.

None of that was for Jessica.

She left her parent's rural Sussex County, New Jersey home at 18 to attend UCLA as a music major. Jessica was never the *Hollywood-type.* She was aware that her talent as a pianist was what she had going for her. That, and the fact that her friends and family considered Jessica to be honest, reliable, trustworthy and a genuinely good person. Between her job, her husband, her piano and their apartment, Jessica had everything she wanted and needed.

Valentina's regulars began applauding as soon as they heard the first few notes of "*Come Back To Sorrento,*" one of the performer's favorite songs. A few patrons danced in the area between the piano and tables, happily dropping fives, tens and twenties into the large brandy snifter Jessica used for tips. Yet, to the lady at the keyboard, the money didn't matter as much as entertaining those who enjoyed her talent, though she was also grateful to average $325 per night.

As she played, Jessica imagined Dean Martin coolly crooning along in Italian, and though she didn't understand a word he sang, she grinned from ear to ear.

Visiting Italy had been Jessica's dream since her teens, and she was anxiously looking forward to the three-week vacation of five Italian cities she and Leon had booked for the end of the upcoming summer.

Jessica was happy to fill her five-hour stints with a never-ending repertoire from her leather folio filled with sheet music to fit every mood, holiday, occasion…*anything.* As the patrons danced, their smiles and excitement kept her from being eager for her eleven o'clock finale.

For the last four years it had been the same routine when she completed her shift. After saying "Good night" to Charlie, Constance and the staff, she would head home, rarely encountering traffic at that hour. The 405 North flowed to the 118 West, and within 20 to 25 minutes of stepping from Valentina's, Jessica would exit at DeSoto Avenue, turn right onto Devonshire Street, left on Independence Avenue and right onto Lemarsh Street, where she and her husband lived in their second floor two-bed-two-bath apartment in the suburban neighborhood of Chatsworth, tucked against the Santa Susana and San Gabriel Mountains in the northwest corner of the San Fernando Valley.

When entering the apartment and walking into the large living room, the first thing one would see was Jessica's Baldwin baby grand in the far corner. It had been a high school graduation present from her parents. On one of the walls behind it were framed photographs and paintings of Italian art, landscapes and landmarks that surrounded a framed UCLA diploma embossed with "Degree of Music," and the name "Jessica Ross" inscribed in calligraphy.

The other wall held a dozen pictures of the happy couple.

Off the tasteful and well-appointed living room were the kitchen and dining room, each furnished and decorated in what was considered the standard "San Fernando Valley functional." Down the left hall was one of the bathrooms and the guest bedroom. At the end of the right hallway was the master suite.

Jessica always said it was thanks to Sylvia, the Farber's 47-year-old housekeeper, who kept the apartment looking so great.

Sylvia Estrada had come from Guatemala more than a quarter of a century earlier to escape poverty and the too-often kidnapping, raping and murdering of her small town's women by gangs, cartels and the local police. In 1987, it took the 20-year-old nine weeks to arduously and perilously make the 2,600-mile journey. Sylvia never spoke of what she had to do to complete the trip, but the moment she crossed from Mexico into southern California, she vowed never to return to her home country again.

Quickly learning English and earning a high school diploma, Sylvia began cleaning homes, and within four years hired several Guatemalan women to work for her. It wasn't long before she acquired influential and famous clients along Mulholland Drive, from Hollywood to Bel Air. One of her early clients was a Pasadena accountant named Michael Pincus, twenty-six years older than her, single, and happy to help the smart, attractive, dark-haired woman with her books as her burgeoning business continued to grow.

In 1996, they married.

Michael was 55. Sylvia was 29.

Their first decade was very enjoyable. They each earned a good living. They traveled repeatedly to Europe and the Caribbean. They dined out often. But Michael's friends and family had always looked down on the much younger Guatemalan housecleaner, and it became a constant issue between the couple. An issue that worsened over the following years.

During that time, Michael became less interested in sex and Sylvia entered her prime.

As a successful business owner, she wanted to experience the best and most decadent that America had to offer, and being in L.A., the options were unlimited for the once-innocent girl from the outskirts of Guatemala City.

Sylvia began to have affairs with men, but more often with women, and had come to enjoy sex in a variety of combinations.

No one could say that the 47-year-old wasn't exceptionally fit and sexually attractive for her age. She kept in shape by actively working with her team of employees, and by going to a Woodland Hills gym to diligently exercise…and to meet younger men and women to discreetly satisfy her needs and desires once or twice a week. She had grown tired of her out-of-shape, unexciting, much older husband.

It was an evening at the gym in December of 2011 when Sylvia crossed paths with a then 29-year old Leon Farber while Jessica was in Brentwood working. A few weeks later Leon had his first threesome with his new friend and one of her girlfriends.

A short time later he recommended to Jessica that they get a cleaning lady. Since they were each earning money, and most of the neighbors already had someone coming to clean *their* homes, she agreed.

Of course, Sylvia's resume and referrals were impeccable, and she made sure the price was right.

A couple of weeks later, the Farbers scheduled Sylvia and one of her employees to arrive every Thursday around three o'clock.

Jessica would be home until five o'clock, just as Leon returned from work, and always made sure his dinner was prepared and ready for him. Then she'd go to Valentina's. Soon after, Sylvia's helper would depart...leaving her boss with Leon to get paid for their services.

As Jessica was finishing "*Return To Me*" to the applause and appreciation of the restaurant's clientele, Leon was fucking their once-a-week housekeeper and one of her female playmates in the Chatsworth guest bedroom...as they had done practically every other Thursday for the last couple of years.

He had always been wise enough to wear condoms during these encounters, and no one knew how to clean up the mess better than Sylvia...and be gone well before Jessica left Valentina's.

CHAPTER 2
Every Dream Comes To An End

It was Monday evening, May 12th, around five o'clock...just another day in the quiet suburban Chatsworth neighborhood of the spacious two-story development that housed the Farbers. The complex looked like many others throughout that end of *The Valley*. Young children played on lawns. The cars along the curb were clean and relatively new. Two mothers walked with strollers while one texted and the other talked on her cell phone.

From an open living room window on the second floor came the enjoyable, melodic and soothing sounds of Jessica's piano.

On the evenings she wasn't at Valentina's, she would often greet her husband's arrival from his eight hours at the office with his favorite songs, mostly because she loved seeing the smile on his face when he entered. She would always have a glass of wine waiting for him on the dining table which was already set for the dinner she was preparing.

But that day when Leon opened the living room door as his wife was playing *"Come Back To Sorrento,"* a song they joked about because of Jessica's attraction and fascination with Italy, Leon wasn't smiling.

His happy partner couldn't help but see it...and her fingers stopped.

"Jess...I want to talk to you."

For the next 20 minutes Jessica sat on the sofa as her husband stood, though mostly paced, before her and calmly explained that he found their marriage unexciting, and that he was no longer attracted to her. Though he never mentioned Sylvia and the two-plus year affair they had been having, he said he wanted to experience more than what he felt Jessica would be willing to consider, and in the end he put the blame on her, saying it was because she wasn't home until 11:30PM four nights a week.

Jessica barely spoke and tried to comprehend words she never thought she'd hear in her life...words that were coming from her husband, her partner, her best friend. She was too confused to cry. Leon had *never* said a word about them having problems with *anything...especially* about her job at Valentina's. He enjoyed the free food and drinks whenever he'd stop by, and he never complained about the $1,300 in cash his wife brought home every week.

It was even more confusing to Jessica to find that Leon had already made up his mind once he said he would stay in the guest room until he could find an apartment.

She went into the kitchen to turn off the oven and the burners under the pots simmering atop the stove, then walked into their bedroom, gently closed the door and cried as she never cried before while staring at the walls and trying to understand what just happened. A few minutes before eight o'clock she stood at the west-facing window to watch the setting sun, then laid on the bed fully dressed and cried until she fell asleep.

For the next seven weeks, life was anything but happy in the Farbers' apartment.

Leon moved his clothes into the guest room and would come home late on the nights Jessica didn't work.

Charlie noticed a lull in the pianist's usual enthusiasm and performance. But Jessica wouldn't talk about it. She *couldn't* talk about it. She didn't understand it herself.

Meanwhile, Sylvia and a helper continued to clean the Farbers' apartment every Thursday.

By the time Leon drove away in a rented truck containing his possessions on Tuesday, July 1ˢᵗ, Jessica had already been served divorce papers. There wasn't much to split. They had no children or outside assets. They divided what was in their IRAs, joint savings and checking accounts. Since their cars were separately owned and paid for, all they had to do was deal with the insurance.

Jessica's father had passed away nine years earlier, and her mom died three years later. She was now on her own and had to take care of herself. Yet, always in the back of her mind were the unanswered questions of, "*Why?* Why didn't he tell me he was unhappy? What was it that he wanted me to do?"

Leon had never complained about their sex life, which was consistent and fulfilling up until the week before he dropped the bomb on his wife. He had always satisfied Jessica, and she was happy to do the same for him in whatever way he wanted. They had been that way since college and throughout their six years of marriage.

When Sylvia and her assistant arrived that Thursday at three o'clock, Jessica sorrowfully paid the cleaning lady and told her she could no longer afford her services. Sylvia acted shocked, took the money and was gone by 3:07PM.

By six o'clock, Sylvia and Leon were in a local motel room... paid for with Jessica's money.

From Sunday, August 10 to Sunday the 31ˢᵗ, no one saw or heard from Jessica. She had requested the three weeks off from Valentina's months earlier when the Farbers were planning to be on Jessica's dream vacation to Italy. She sequestered herself in the apartment, mostly on her bed watching TV...and didn't go near her piano until September 1ˢᵗ.

It was 64 degrees at 5:20PM on Tuesday, February 17ᵗʰ, 2015, and in another twenty minutes the sun would fall below the horizon.

Jessica, having turned 32 a month earlier, had the living room windows open as the neighbors listened to her piano. They didn't have a clue that she was now playing to keep herself occupied… and to keep herself sane. In her mind, it was the eight-month anniversary of answering the apartment door to be served divorce papers.

Her auburn hair was now five inches longer. The room looked the same as it had several months earlier. The same pictures adorned the walls behind the piano. Besides her normal schedule at Valentina's, Jessica had begun teaching students in the apartment to cover the bills.

Her eyes reflected recent tears. She closed them as she played songs from memory that were note-for-note-perfect. Without pause, she opened a book of music and didn't allow her eyes to stray from its pages in order to avoid looking at the suitcase standing near the same dreaded apartment door.

That was when the house phone rang.

Jessica kept playing.

It rang again.

She glanced at the Caller ID on the handset resting atop the piano, which caused her fingers to falter. Her playing awkwardly slowed…then stopped.

Quickly looking to the window to see the last rays of the sun, Jessica raised the phone on its fourth ring and softly answered.

"Hello?"

She listened to Leon's voice and replied, "Yes, I'm okay."

He asked why she had called him at work earlier that day.

It was hard for her to speak, but she forced herself.

"You…you still had a few things here. I found them in our…" She caught herself making the same mistake she had been making in conversations over the last several months. She mentally cursed herself, held back tears, then took a quick breath and continued, "…*my* closet. I put them in a suitcase. I…I think that's the last of it."

Listening to what he had to say, she began to sob…but as hard as it was, she controlled herself. She did *not* want him to hear her crumble…more than she already had.

"Okay," she said. "I'll put it outside in a few minutes."

He thanked her and hung up before she could say "Bye."

In a rage of anger and humiliation unlike her, Jessica burst into tears as she threw the receiver across the room onto the sofa and pounded her hands onto the piano's keys…making a horrendous sound to anyone within earshot of the open window. Hitting her beloved instrument was something Jessica had never done, and it angered her even more.

She abruptly stood, stomped to the front door, opened it and shoved the suitcase outside. Slamming the door closed, she rushed to her bathroom and proceeded to get on her knees and vomit into the toilet bowl.

It was a good 30 minutes after Jessica had thrown up what little was in her stomach before she cleaned the vomit residue from inside and around the bowl, and finally…from her face. She brushed her teeth and gargled…she wanted to get the taste of puke, and Leon, out of her mouth.

After changing her blouse, which suffered the effects of the toilet's water splashing back, Jessica made her way into the kitchen to pour herself a glass of wine. Through the open living room window she heard footsteps approaching the apartment.

Against her better judgement, she quietly rushed to the door and looked through the peephole to see Leon walk straight to the suitcase, pick it up, turn and walk away.

Though tears were running down her face, she held back any sound. As his footsteps grew faint and he was no longer visible, Jessica pressed her face against the door, slid to the floor and let her emotions out.

Two nights later, Jessica sat behind Valentina's baby grand playing with an energy and attitude that had been lost over the last few months. Since watching Leon pick up the suitcase, she had cried enough to make her realize that she had to accept the reality that her life had changed. He was gone, and she either had to restart her life...or live in a cardboard box under the 10 Freeway talking to herself and strangers about the questions she never was able to get answers to.

One person who helped give Jessica several emotional slaps in the face was her friend, 28-year-old Suzanne Ariza, a bubbly, cute bundle of energy and caffeine with natural blonde hair that Jessica always admired.

Suzanne was sitting at the bar nursing a peppermint schnapps while giving her support to Jessica before leaving to sing with her band Two Ton Sun at The Zone, which was one of the currently trendy rock clubs in West Hollywood on Sunset Blvd. If there was a complete opposite in the clientele and the music of Valentina's... it was The Zone's.

The patrons must have especially enjoyed Jessica's playing that night because the brandy snifter atop the piano was filled to the brim with tens and twenties...and it was only 8:45PM.

Needing to be dressed and on stage at ten o'clock, Suzanne left a few minutes later, but not before going to the ladies room, then passing the piano to give a 'thumbs up' and wink to Jessica prior to heading out the door.

Like clockwork, Jessica finished the last set at eleven o'clock with "Stardust" to a round of applause from those still there, but before she could close the lid over the keys, she felt a man's hand on her shoulder. She looked up the well-dressed arm to see the familiar face of Charlie.

He had an odd, forced smile. It was one she had never seen during their nearly five-year friendship. He didn't say anything. He just cocked his head, indicating she was to follow him, which she did.

As they walked through the kitchen, Charlie gave the same signal to Constance, who stopped what she was doing to join them.

When they entered his office, he sat on the edge of his desk, indicating that the ladies should sit on the sofa that flanked the wall. Charlie's forced smile turned to a frown, his unhappiness was evident as his head dropped to his chest.

Jessica tried to lighten the atmosphere by cheerfully asking, "What's up, Charlie? You look a little stressed."

His face rose just enough to make eye contact with her as he answered, "The restaurant's been sold, Jess."

Simultaneously, the two women yelled, "*What?*" then looked in shock at one another, and then back to Charlie.

He stood up and made his way to a cabinet behind the desk as he said, "I got the call about fifteen minutes ago. Looks like the three of us, and everyone else in the place except the busboys, are out on our asses."

Unable to hide her desperation, Jessica blurted out, "Can we work for the new owners?"

Charlie opened the cabinet, took out a bottle of Rémy Martin and three snifters. He delayed answering as he poured the fine cognac and handed one to each of the now-stunned-and-speechless women.

Returning to his spot on the edge of the desk, he looked at them as he spoke.

"They're not gonna need a pianist, a gourmet chef…or me. Some young rich kids are making it a sports-bar-and-sushi-joint with TVs coverin' every wall. Not much call for people like us. We'll be okay for another few weeks, 'til April first. After that…" he looked down into his snifter and finished with, "Sorry."

Jessica's eyes filled with tears.

"Hey…what's the matter, Jess?" came from Constance, the more-than-slightly overweight 58-year-old culinary artiste in a city of culinary artistes…with most of them younger and willing to work for half or two-thirds her price. "You're talented. You're young. You'll get another job. Me? Charlie? At our age? Where the fuck are *we* gonna go? You? You'll be fine."

Constance held up her glass and waited for the others to do the same. Then, in their best Italian flair, the three complimented themselves with a proud, "Saluti!"

As each drank to the toast, their eyes looked distant…unsure of what their individual futures held.

In the nearly five years Jessica had worked at Valentina's, that was the first time she arrived home after midnight. Not only did she have a tearful "Goodnight" with Constance and Charlie, her anxiety-filled mind resulted in her missing the exit off the 405 North, causing her to drive an extra twelve miles to get to the 118 West.

Reaching the front door, with her key ready to enter the lock, she looked at the label above the bell that read, "Leon & Jessica Farber."

It hurt to look at it…so she ripped off the "Leon &," tore it in half, crumpled it and threw it on the walkway, then she went inside.

She had just lost her job of playing the piano and performing for people. It was her job that was keeping Jessica sane.

It was also the major component for covering her bills. On top of everything else, Jessica was now paying a divorce attorney.

It only took a few moments to drop her purse and jacket on the sofa, walk into her bedroom, throw herself face-first onto the mattress and cry into her pillow.

In too short of a period in her life, just nine months, Jessica had lost her best friend…her husband…and now her job. The two things in Jessica's life that she cherished the most.

CHAPTER 3
Havin' A Good Time, Pammie?

Outside of one of the more-than-a-dozen non-franchised coffee shops along Chatsworth's Devonshire Street sat Suzanne and Jessica. It was Friday, March 20th, and a comfortable 72 degrees made it just another beautiful day in the San Fernando Valley.

Jessica unhurriedly enjoyed her iced coffee and being out of the apartment. Suzanne had already sucked down her second...with each containing two shots of espresso, so it was no surprise that she controlled the conversation.

"What the fuck are you worried about, Jess? There's *tons* of classy joints from Hollywood to Malibu, and down to Long Beach, Newport and Laguna. Not like the places *I* play. You got the look, the clothes...you've even got that bullshit 'between song banter' down."

Jessica brought the straw to her mouth and gave some thought to what her friend had just said, then lowered her drink. The enjoyment she was temporarily feeling disappeared as she answered, "And none of them are looking. They all have their regular pianists or small groups that they've been using for years...just like I had been at Valentina's."

Trying to stay positive, Suzanne came back with, "C'mon, Jess, you're great! You'll get a job in no time."

"They're closing in two more weeks," Jessica quickly retorted, then shook her head and continued, "All I have are four kids who come over for lessons once a week, and they're not gonna cover the bills. Plus, their attention span for practicing and reading the damn notes on the page is non-existent…and half the time their hands are sticky and it gets on my keys." Jessica put her iced coffee down and started waving her hands around as she spoke, "It's like their parents are paying me to babysit them for an hour. They have no interest in their kids' progress, and I doubt they make them practice at home. Drives me *nuts!*"

Suzanne caught a glimpse of Jessica's left hand and blurted out, "What the fuck is with the wedding ring?" Her volume rose to a level that made it easy for the people at the next table to hear. "It's *over!* It's *done!*" Suzanne belted out in her rock vocalist bellow. "He left 'cause he said he wanted 'more excitement' in his fuckin' life, for Christsake. He said 'you're boring' and then he fuckin' left! Sell the friggin' ring and pay your rent for a couple of months. *Fuck him! Fuck him, Jess!*"

Because of the reaction of those at the surrounding tables, Suzanne lowered her voice enough to keep their conversation private, "And the pictures of the two of you behind the piano… what the fuck's with *that?*"

Jessica cowered and sorrowfully said, "I know, Suz. But…"

"But *what?*"

"I…somewhere inside me…I think I still love him," Jessica answered, holding back tears.

"*No you don't!* You still love what you *had.* You still love the *memories.* Get the fucking past out of your head and start making some *new* memories. That's all you have to do! I know *tons* of guys. You want me to set you up with one or two?"

Jessica looked at Suzanne with appreciation and trust in her eyes, then used her paper napkin to sop up the tears now trickling down her face as she said, "Thanks…but no, Suz. Let me deal with one thing at a time. I have to find a job, otherwise I'll have to find a new place to live, and to do that, I may have to sell my piano. And I can't. I just can *not* do that. *Ever!*"

The realization of having to sell her piano and actually saying the words out loud made the tears run even faster.

"That prick really fucked you up," Suzanne angrily shouted, again garnering a glare from the people at the next table. "We gotta get you back on your feet. You've got to stop thinking about him and move the fuck on."

"Easier said than done, Suz." Jessica lowered her head and painfully said, "If my folks *were* alive…this would've killed them."

The young blonde had no response.

Trying to lighten the mood, Jessica brought her iced coffee's straw to her mouth, sucked down the last of the liquid and chuckled, "You know…maybe I should move somewhere. Start over."

Suzanne chuckled equally in return, "Let me guess…Italy, right?"

"Ever since I was a kid, I'd dream about what it must be like. The art, the history, the ruins, the food…" then, smiling again, she finished her thought, "…the men. *Italian* men."

"Yeah, well, I hear that's the best place to find 'em." Suzanne finished her espresso-filled iced coffee and jokingly asked, "Jess, I've known you for a few years now, and to the best of my knowledge, you've never been there, right?"

Jessica shook her head.

"And you don't speak Italian, right? You know, more than just 'Buon giorno' and 'Grazie.'"

Jessica shook her head…and smiled.

"So that means you don't have any friends in Italy, right?"

Jessica shook her head, still smiling and appreciating Suzanne's companionship and humor.

"So," Suzanne continued, "You've got no money, never been there, don't speak the language, and no one to show you the ropes. You haven't given this much thought, have you?"

Jessica stood, picked up her purse from the table and answered with resolve, "You're right. It's a crazy idea." She tossed her container into the trash receptacle, looked at her cheery, over-caffeinated friend and said, "C'mon, let's go."

It wasn't long after Jessica returned to the apartment that she took off the wedding ring and put it in her jewelry case, though it hurt to do so. The next possessions to go were the photographs of the 'happy couple' on the wall. But after a few minutes of playing the piano without having Leon's image near her…it felt good.

Only her UCLA diploma and the pictures of Italy remained.

Somewhere around 3:30PM, Jessica sat on the sofa with a telephone handset and sadly circled the only two "Pianist Wanted" ads she could find on a jobsite.

She dialed, but her frazzled nerves caused her finger to hit a wrong digit. Hanging up, Jessica took a deep breath and gave it another try.

It rang once.

A recording answered.

She sat through the message, then…*Beep*.

Jessica realized she was so nervous and anxious, she had no idea what to say…and never thought to hang up.

"Uh…hello. My name is Jessica Farb--"

Flustered, she quickly looked at the diploma behind the piano and started over. "My name is Jessica *Ross*. I'm calling about the ad, *your* ad, er…for a pianist. I, uhm…I've been working at Valentina's in Brentwood for nearly five years. They were sold recently and--"

Beep.

Frustrated, she hung up, shook her head, scratched out the ad, took another deep breath, picked up the phone and confidently dialed the next number.

It rang, a recording answered, then…*Beep*.

In her most professional voice, she began, "Hello. My name is Jessica Ross. For the last five years I've been the pianist at Valentina's. I'd like to set up an audition."

She left her home and cell numbers and felt good about how she handled her message, though regretted not doing the same with the first call.

After making dinner for herself, she showered, dressed and left for work at five o'clock.

Sunday, March 29th was Valentina's last night of business. The place was jammed. *All* the regulars were there. Charlie didn't lock the door until the last customer left at 1:30AM. Constance cooked everything that was in the kitchen and had the servers bring complimentary appetizers and finger food throughout the night. Jessica didn't play the last note of music until Charlie locked the door…mostly because she didn't want the night to end.

As the restaurant's employees cleaned up for the last time, the three friends gathered in Charlie's office to finish his bottle of Rémy Martin…then locked the front door for good just after three in the morning, before heading to their cars.

Driving cautiously, Jessica was home by 3:30AM…and asleep a few minutes later.

It was Saturday night around 10:30PM on May 30th, and the stress of not finding a job, plus the weight of constant legal fees and some unpaid bills were taking their toll on Jessica. She wasn't sleeping much, and it was beginning to show in her appearance. It was only because Suzanne put Jessica's name on The Zone's guest list, thus avoiding the $15 cover charge, that the out-of-work pianist, noticeably out of place in her attire, found herself at the bar nursing a bottle of beer.

It was the usual packed house for a Saturday night, plus, Suzanne's group had a loyal following. At the moment, she was onstage, mid-song, with a tight four-piece group of rockers behind her. The two guitarists, bassist and drummer had formed Two Ton Sun with Suzanne three years earlier and were now regulars on Sunset Blvd and in every other club that could afford them.

When the song ended and the applause started, the DJ's voice boomed through the speakers from his booth as the group left the stage

"Ladies and gentlemen! That was The Zone's number one band! *Two...Ton...Sun!*"

That brought more applause.

The DJ tapped a button causing recorded music to fill the club...which drove people to the dance floor.

Sweaty as she passed through friends, fans and strangers, Suzanne made her way to Jessica, grabbed her beer, gulped a couple of mouthfuls and said, "Thanks. I needed that."

Jessica watched Suzanne put the near empty bottle on the bar, then said, "Yeah, so I see."

Over the music, Suzanne instructed Jessica to follow her backstage to the dressing room.

They were happy to find it empty, but the beat of the bass still vibrated through the walls as they spoke.

Suzanne asked, "Find a job yet?"

Uncomfortable because she hadn't, Jessica put a different spin on the conversation by answering, "You know, Suz...this place is like your second home. Don't you need a piano player in the band?"

Suzanne laughed as she answered, "Think you'd fit in?" gesturing to her friend's straight clothes and appearance.

Getting the rocker's point, Jessica sighed and gave in.

"Then the answer's 'No...I didn't find a job.'"

Suzanne sat on the worn couch and said, "Shit, Jess...it's been two months." She had Jessica sit next to her as a grin came across her face. "Listen...I know about a job. A friend of mine works there. She said they're gonna need someone to answer the phone. It's not too artistic, but from what I understand, it pays well. *Real* well."

Jessica was both happy and cautiously intrigued as she asked, "*How* well?"

Suzanne replied, "I bet it's enough to cover your bills. And that's all that matters right now, right?"

"For answering a phone?"

"At some classy massage parlor," Suzanne said, getting right to the point.

Jessica's mouth and eyes opened wide…unsure of what to say, so Suzanne, laughing at her reaction, kept going.

"Easy, Mother Teresa. This girl I know, Pam…she works for this guy who owns a few of them. She says they're top-of-the-line places. She only answers the phone, no massage stuff…and she's movin' to Mexico, so they need somebody to replace her."

Jessica asked the first question that came to mind.

"Is it legal?"

"I don't see why not. They just give the customer…" Suzanne made her voice sound sarcastically erotic. "…a *sensual* massage."

"Sensual?"

"Look…all you gotta do is set up the appointments. It's easy. Consider it a temp-job until something better comes along. Then quit."

Not wanting to hurt her friend's feelings, Jessica respectfully replied, "Thanks, Suz, I really appreciate you trying to help, but I don't think so."

As the two women stood to leave, Suzanne said with sincerity, "Look, the final decision is up to you. But if nothing better comes along in a few weeks and your back's against the wall with bills… let me know."

Jessica gave Suzanne an appreciative heartfelt hug. Back at the bar they exchanged cheek kisses before the unemployed pianist left to make the drive over Coldwater Canyon to the 101 Freeway that would take her to the 405 North, and eventually to Chatsworth.

Once home, all she had to worry about, as she had for the past few months, was to get a good night's sleep.

A little after 8:30PM on Tuesday, June 2nd, the sun dipped below the Pacific Ocean's horizon and the full moon glistened off the nearly-still water only 37 miles from Puerto Vallarta, Mexico… where the Bahia De Banderas, the Bay of Flags, met the open sea.

The 38' motorboat calmly floated as Martha Reeves & The Vandellas' "*Heat Wave*" blasted through its speakers. Its engines were off and only the cockpit and running lights were on. There wasn't another boat in sight.

Suzanne and a drunken 31-year-old Pamela Sorel, both wearing bikinis, were dancing on the rear deck. As the song ended, the women laughed and walked to a small table where they sat to do shots of tequila and each snorted two lines of cocaine off a mirror.

Wiping the residual powder from her nose, Suzanne happily grinned at her friend and asked, "Havin' a good time, Pammie?"

There was no verbal answer, just a wide grin as Pamela filled their two shot glasses and slammed back one of them.

Suzanne's smile was replaced with an angry glare as she probed, "So…" Pamela looked at Suzanne and wondered why her facial expression had changed as the question continued. "Why did you take his money?"

Pamela, alarmed, was trying to think of a viable answer as a gloved left hand came from behind and held her body. Then…a gloved right hand, gripping a large knife, slit her throat.

A powerful cascade of blood shot across the table onto Suzanne. She screamed as Pamela's body jerked hard several times…then went limp.

"*Why did you do that?*" Suzanne yelled, knowing no one could hear or see them.

Dropping the blood-covered weapon on the table, the gloved hands dragged the dead, bleeding body to the edge of the boat's port side as the shocked Suzanne continue to yell, "We were just supposed to scare her and get the money back! *Not kill her! Oh my god!*"

Pamela's corpse was dropped into the salt water as blood flowed from the neck's open gash with the moon reflecting around it. Suzanne watched the body float for only a moment before it quickly and quietly slipped below the surface.

The engines started as Jimi Hendrix's *"Purple Haze"* came through the speakers. Then the boat turned to begin the long trip to its dock in the Marina Vallarta.

Still in shock, Suzanne removed her blood soaked bikini top and threw it in the water, then, while still topless, she went below for paper towels and cleaning products to rid the table and knife of any indication of what had just taken place…and any trace of Pam's DNA. After she finished and tossed all the evidence overboard, she unraveled a short hose to wash the blood from the rear deck and watched the reddish water flow into the scuppers…then into the ocean. She snorted 4 large lines from the mirror, then walked to the bow and laid down in the moonlight…trying to forget what she had just witnessed.

Two weeks later, Jessica was grateful that it was too warm to open the windows as the apartment's central air-conditioning kept the sound of a poorly played song coming from her piano inside. She didn't want the neighbors, who were used to hearing the most wonderfully performed melodies, to hear what was now being played.

Still not sleeping throughout the night, Jessica was sitting on the piano bench next to 9-year-old Carol, one of her pupils. The child was reading from a lesson book and Jessica was trying her best to be supportive, but cringed at every bad note the young fingers hit.

"All right, let's try it again."

Carol tried, but there was no improvement the second time around.

A light knock on the door caused Jessica to look at the clock, bringing a grateful smile to her face as she called out, "Come in!"

Carol's mother entered and watched from across the room as her daughter continued to play what should have been a recognizable song. She, too, cringed at every bad note.

Once the child finished, she looked at her mother. The mother, in turn, disappointedly looked at Jessica, who could only say, "We're making progress."

Walking to the piano, the mother handed Jessica a check and asked, "Same time next week?"

Nodding, the teacher returned with, "I'm pretty open if you'd like to have her come twice a week. It may help."

"Well, we'll keep that in mind," came the kind response. "C'mon, honey."

Carol slid off the bench and walked out with her mom. That was Jessica's cue to open the top of the bench, reach in for a spray bottle of 409 and paper towels, then wipe down the keys.

Twice.

It was only a short time later that Jessica sat at the dining room table looking over some job-site printouts with circles around various possibilities…though none were for pianists. She stared at them, then looked in the center of the table at the pile of bills.

She grabbed the house-phone, dialed and waited for an answer.

"Suz…remember you said something about a job answering phones?" She listened to her friend's response, then said, "Let's go for coffee. Your treat."

CHAPTER 4
Must Be Quite The Rubdown

Driving straight through Chatsworth and Woodland Hills along Topanga Canyon Blvd, Jessica followed her car's GPS to the two-floor Calabasas office complex on the border of the Greater Mulwood section, which is the triangle between Old Topanga Canyon Road, Mulholland Drive and Mulholland Highway.

Though it was only nine miles from door-to-door, due to the lights and *The Valley's* traffic, it took 35 minutes. She was five minutes early for her 1:30PM report time…and only one day after having coffee with Suzanne.

Surprised that a massage parlor would be on Mulholland Highway, which was nothing more than a scenic two-lane road, Jessica found it even more amusing that a few minutes away were Elementary, Middle and High Schools, The Performance Arts Education Center, the Montessori pre-school, the Chabad of Calabasas, and an equestrian center. If she wanted, Jessica could take a handful of routes from here and be at several Malibu beaches in twenty-to-thirty minutes.

The 24,000 residents of Calabasas were proud of the town's location in between Malibu and The Valley, with those calling their southern border residences "Malibu-adjacent."

Pulling into the large open-air parking lot, Jessica, dressed in the business attire one would wear when interviewing for a new job, looked at the other businesses in the complex and saw they were much nicer than similar locations.

It wasn't hard to find Suite 16 due to its elegant brass plaque that was etched with the words *Diamond Jim's – 2:00PM to 11:00PM.*

She tried to push the heavy wooden door open, but it was locked.

Spotting the doorbell under the nameplate, she pressed it. A few seconds later the door opened and Jessica was greeted by Debbie, a striking beauty in her late 20s wearing a stylish nurse's outfit, complete with a starched white cap and tight-fitting top. She stood about 5'10 without heels…though the ones she was wearing brought her to over 6'. But it was her well-built body with larger-than-normal implants that stunned Jessica at first glance.

Staring at Debbie's nipples that protruded through the tight white blouse, which were practically eye-level and appeared to be pointing directly at her, Jessica was speechless.

"Like 'em, don'tcha?" the 'nurse' asked, with a twinge of humor and sensuality.

"Uh…" was all Jessica could get out.

"The new phone girl, right?" Debbie asked, with a smile that never left her face.

Forcing her eyes to move up to Debbie's, Jessica apprehensively responded with, "I'm Jessica Ross. Volpe sent me. But…how did you know who I was?"

Debbie pointed to the video camera above them.

"We knew you were coming. You're not one of the girls who work here, and it's too early for our customers…so I took a shot," then she extended a hand in greeting as Jessica heard, "Hi! I'm Debbie." The nurse held open the door and led the new employee directly into the voluminous, well-lit reception area containing the large oak desk where Jessica was told, "This'll be where you sit."

As the door closed behind them, Jessica heard an electronic lock secure it.

There were two tasteful sofas facing each other separated by an ornate coffee table in the center of the room, and four comfortable cushioned chairs surrounded a small oak table neatly stacked with an assortment of sports and current events magazines. Below the large, muted HDTV on the far wall stood a full bar and an attractive Asian bartender. There was also soft, relaxing music playing through unseen speakers.

On the desk sat a three-line office phone, complete with a credit card reader and receipt printer built into it, a 36-inch closed circuit screen showing seven video feeds, and a button built into the desk next to the phone that would electronically unlock the front door. There was no computer.

There were two video cameras outside. One faced the parking lot and the other faced the front door. Inside, one faced the entrance to watch clients come and go, one covered the reception area, one captured the hall from the locker room to the treatment rooms, another captured the hallway from the treatment rooms to the reception area, and the last was strategically placed in the office.

There were two closed doors behind the receptionist's desk. One was the employees' bathroom. The other led into the office.

Of the two doors next to the bar, one led the clients to separate male and female locker rooms complete with gender-appropriate attendants, showers, bathrooms, steam rooms and saunas…and with every amenity required. When they were ready, the client would slip on clean rubber sandals, wrap themselves in a towel and the attendant, via an intercom, would call the assigned therapist. The therapist would arrive to escort the client down the hallway to one of the eight treatment rooms, and then return them to their appropriate locker room after their session. Each room had its own décor, lights, music and was twice the size of similar businesses. Other than the emergency exit at the end of the hallway, there were no windows.

The second door by the bar was for the therapists. It was the hallway to-and-from the treatment rooms they would use to come into the reception area.

Diamond Jim's was unlike any place Jessica had ever been in, or had ever *imagined* she'd be in. Additionally, it was nothing like she envisioned such a place would be. The spacious setting and the décor of the reception area calmed her, as did the fact that everything was spotlessly clean.

Debbie stood Jessica in front of the desk and introduced her to the two people sitting across from each other on the sofas as Jessica took a resume from her purse.

Darryl Bowling was in his mid-30s, black, just under six feet tall and muscular. He was dressed in pressed designer jeans, a collared shirt, was well-spoken and very personable. There was an air about Darryl that made people feel comfortable when they met him.

Patricia was 29, coiffed long dark brown hair, very attractive and stood about an inch or two above Jessica's 5'7. Jessica noticed Patricia was also wearing a business suit, only hers was more stylish, current and expensive than her own. It was all giving Jessica a self-conscious feeling that she couldn't be more out of place.

While making small talk with Darryl, Patricia was drawing on the page of a large sketchpad.

Pointing to her co-workers as if they needed to be told apart, Debbie said, "This is Darryl, and this is Patty. She's one of the therapists."

The artist put the pad aside, stood, offered her hand and cordially said, "It's Patricia. Nice to meet you."

As the two were shaking hands, Debbie continued with, "This is Jennifer."

Darryl stood and extended his hand as the new employee told them, "It's Jessica."

Debbie threw up her hands and laughed, "Whatever!"

"It's a pleasure," came from Darryl.

Unsure who he was and seeing that he was with Patricia, Jessica assumed he was a patron, so she tried to be professional by smiling and answering, "Thank you. Are you a client?"

The three laughed as Darryl answered, "No. We don't open for another half-hour or so. Debbie'll show you around first. I'm here for *you*."

A little freaked by his words, Jessica retorted, "I'm sorry, but I'm not a masseuse."

"Yeah, I know that, honey," he replied. "I'm 'Security.'"

His answer stunned her as she asked, "*Security?*" Jessica looked at Patricia and questioned, "I'll need *security?*"

Debbie interjected, "He's here in *case* you need him. Nothing's ever happened before."

Darryl winked and joked, "Except that one time a few months ago. Remember that?"

Patricia tried to calm the tension, "Cut it out, you two. Don't scare her."

Darryl went into the top drawer of the desk and took out a fob with two buttons on it. He handed it to Jessica, then instructed her to, "Keep it close. If I'm not here and someone bothers you, just press this green button," then he pointed to the red button under it and said, "This one shuts it off."

"Shuts *what* off?" Jessica nervously asked.

"An alarm that'll scare the shit outta whoever's bothering you… and they'll run. Trust me," interjected Debbie again.

Jessica gave a worried look to Patricia and exclaimed, "And you told *him* not to scare me?"

"It also alerts me and the police," Darryl threw in, with hopes of calming Jessica's apprehension.

As he returned to his spot on the sofa, Debbie handed Jessica a sheet of paper and began her rundown of the new job.

That was when Jessica handed Debbie her resume.

"What's this?" the nurse asked.

"My resume," Jessica innocently replied.

"Honey," Darryl chuckled, "You don't need one. Whoever vouched for you, and the fact that you're here, means you already got the job."

Laying the resume on the coffee table, Debbie pointed to the paper in Jessica's hand and said, "It's a script. It's what you say when you answer the phone. The majority of the callers will be our 'regulars,' so you won't have to do much more than let them know who's working and what times are available. Just remember, on top of your regular salary, your cut depends on how many people you get in here. There are eight rooms with at least six therapists always on staff, and it's your job to keep the rooms filled and the therapists busy."

Patricia sympathetically eyed Jessica as she reviewed the script and asked, "Ever do anything like this before?"

The novice shook her head, then confirmed, "So when they call…they'll be asking for a massage, right?"

Putting a piece of gum in her mouth, Debbie replied as she began chewing, "Yeah, well, some. Like I said, most are already clients. Some want the same girl, their favorites. Most like to mix it up. The bulk of them have high-stress lives, so they come here for the highest quality rubdown and some relaxation." Then she winked at Jessica and assured her, "Don't worry. You'll get the hang of it."

As Jessica's indoctrination continued, the doorbell would occasionally ring. Either Patricia or Debbie would step behind the desk, look at the video screen, see who it was and tap the button next to the phone to electronically let the therapists and locker room attendants in. After a quick "Hello" and introduction, they passed through the reception area and headed to their stations and treatment rooms.

Darryl felt it was time to pass along some vital information.

"Volpe calls in sometimes just to see how it's goin'. Be honest, 'cause if you're *not*, he gets pissed. You know Volpe."

"Actually, I *don't* know Volpe," Jessica replied. "I got the job through a friend-of-a-friend."

The three employees all let out their own form of laughter at Jessica's words.

Debbie admitted, "I've been here a year and *still* haven't met him. We spoke on the phone a couple of times, but that's it."

Jessica looked at Darryl for *his* knowledge of Volpe. He shook his head and said, "I've worked for him for almost two years. I'm the head of Security for his two other places and never met the guy. All I can say is that the man knows about efficiency and his pay envelopes are always on the money…that's all *I* care about."

Patricia looked up from sketching to offer what she knew of the elusive Volpe. While she spoke, Jessica looked at her. There was something friendly about Patricia's face, the manner in which she expressed herself, and the way she spoke to Jessica. It made the nervous pianist comfortable.

"I got the job through one of the girls, so we never met. I've answered the phone a couple of times when he called, but…" Patricia took a breath and finished with, "That was it."

"What kind of name *is* Volpe?" Jessica asked.

Darryl shrugged and replied with, "A nickname, I guess." That was when his cell phone beeped. He glanced at a text message, then stood up and said, "Gotta run." He eyed Jessica and told her, "Call if you need me. Debbie has the number, so put it in your phone." Then he smiled and winked. "Good havin' ya aboard." He headed for the front door and yelled out, "See y'all later."

The ladies each gave their versions of "Bye!" as Jessica heard the heavy wooden door electronically lock behind him as he departed.

The sound of the lock gave Jessica a feeling of security.

Debbie turned to Jessica and said, "C'mon, I'll show you around. Customers with appointments are gonna start arriving between two and two-thirty, so you're gonna need to know the process."

"The process?" Jessica quickly replied.

Patricia went back to her sketching and said with a wink, "Don't worry. You'll get it. You'll be okay."

The fact that it came from Patricia calmed Jessica a bit.

But just a bit.

The nurse and the trainee walked into the unlocked, large, sparse office. The first thing Jessica noticed was a small, cheap desk at the far end, and that except for the phone resting on it, the room lacked a computer or *any* electronic devices. Nothing decorated the walls except for sixteen framed Certified Massage Therapist certifications from the California Massage Therapy Council, each with a photo of a therapist. It didn't take long for Jessica to find Debbie and Patricia.

Debbie saw Jessica's eyes go to them and said, "Let people say what they want about what we do, but Volpe made sure we had our certifications before we got here, and that we take our thirty-hour Continuing Ed courses to stay current and legitimate."

One wall had a large wooden cabinet housing several compartments, with each one having its own wooden door.

One compartment at eye level contained an old 5-CD player, a power amp, and a stack of CDs used for the music heard in the reception area. Debbie pointed to it and said, "We keep it running all day and night. You can change them whenever you'd like, but Volpe wants it to be background music. No singing. Just music. *Relaxing* music. Nothing wild."

"No problem," Jessica replied, knowing Debbie had no idea of her musical background. Then she sarcastically threw in, "I'll leave my Van Halen catalog at home," which took Debbie by surprise. She couldn't imagine this straightlaced woman in front of her being into *any* heavy metal group, resulting in her giving Jessica an odd look.

To make sure what she said was taken as a joke, the pianist winked and chuckled, "Just kidding."

Debbie feigned fainting and began laughing. Jessica was happy to break the ice with her.

Opening a compartment on the bottom level, Debbie revealed a safe with a keypad and a slot on top. "The customers'll pay you with cash or credit cards when they walk in, and pay their tips when they leave," then emphasized, "Don't *ever* take a check unless you want it comin' out of *your* money." Then Debbie's voice became firm to emphasize what she was about to say. "Above your head on the wall behind you is a camera and it's pointed right at the safe. It sees who comes in this room and who leaves. Remember that." Debbie looked at Jessica to make sure she understood the importance of what was just said.

Jessica raised her eyebrows and nodded to convey she got it.

"Apparently, somebody wasn't putting everything in here like they were supposed to, so Darryl put the camera up a few weeks ago," Debbie said, then continued with, "It's important you log everything in the book."

"The book?"

"There's a new one in your desk. I'll show you. After you log the figures next to the client's name, put the money or the credit card receipts in the slot. Volpe's the only one with the code and I hear he comes by a couple of times a week after we close to clean it out." Debbie reached into her pocket, pulled out a key and said, "It's your job to get here no later than one o'clock to let us in. The locker room attendants have to get things ready, the bartender has to get set up, and the therapists have to prepare their rooms for the clients before they start arriving," then she waved both of her hands along the outline of her body and said with a sexy tilt to her voice, "And some of us have to change into our outfits."

Jessica felt comfortable enough to teasingly ask, "You mean you're not really a nurse?"

Both women laughed loud enough for Patricia to hear them in the reception area. The laughter brought a smile to her naturally pretty face as she read, and was impressed by, Jessica's resume that was left on the coffee table.

Debbie handed Jessica the key, in addition to passing along more information.

"Like I was saying, you start at one o'clock, and close at eleven, Wednesday to Saturday. Even girls like *us* take Sunday's off."

"Forty hours in four days?" Jessica asked.

"Trust me, Jess, your job's easy. Sit that cute little ass behind the desk, answer the phone, log everything in the book, fill in the schedule…and smile for the customers as they come in and leave. We'll take care of the *hard* part. Literally," resulting in them laughing at the pun. "And I'm tellin' you…I doubt you've ever made what you're gonna clear workin' here." It reminded Debbie of something else to tell the new girl. "Your tax paperwork is in the top drawer of the desk. Make sure you fill it out and drop it in the slot for Volpe."

"Taxes? We pay taxes?"

"I'm *tellin' you*…everything here is on the up-and-up," Debbie said with confidence. "We're certified as therapists, we pay taxes, and we get a decent health insurance package. Just don't fuck up or fuck anything up for Volpe and you'll do fine. Now, where the fuck was I?"

"The hours."

Debbie continued, "The last customer has to be out by ten-thirty…and if you can't show up for work for any reason, call Darryl and he'll open up. The only other people I know who have keys are Volpe and Darryl."

Jessica apprehensively asked, "And how much do we--"

Anticipating the question, Debbie got to the point. "On top of your salary you get twenty-points on the tips."

"Points?" Jessica innocently asked.

"Percent. Twenty-percent," she answered without blinking. "The girls get sixty-five percent of the fee, plus sixty percent of the tips. Volpe gets the rest."

"What's a 'rubdown' go for these days?"

"Here? Honey, this ain't one of those forty-buck Chinese rub-and-tug joints. Just to show up they pay two-fifty."

Jessica's face displayed her shock at the price.

Debbie laughed and told the dumbstruck woman, "That's why girls like me, Patricia and the others you'll meet, all want to work in Volpe's places. They're classy. No dives. The high price keeps out the trash, and Volpe makes sure all of us are of a…" she winked at the innocent pianist and finished with, "…certain quality."

Jessica didn't know exactly what Debbie meant, but smiled to give the impression she did.

"And once they're inside, "Debbie continued, "There's no limit to the size of the tip they'll give us."

Catching on, Jessica skeptically said, "Must be quite the rubdown."

With a knowing smile, Debbie returned with, "You got *that* right."

Jessica realized Debbie knew more than the average massage therapist did about her occupation when she said, "Nationally, the average 'take-home' salary-and-tips for a certified massage therapist is around thirty-five grand. In California it's a little more, probably because of the cost of living, but it's around forty. I've been here just over a year and work about fifteen days a month... Wednesdays, Thursdays, Fridays and every other Saturday, and in that time..." Debbie glared at Jessica and said with a laugh, "I've made a hundred and sixty-two grand."

"*What?*" blurted Jessica.

Without missing a beat, Debbie continued, "I hear a few girls at Volpe's other places earned over two-hundred."

As they were leaving the office, Debbie remembered another important aspect of Jessica's responsibilities, "Oh...and keep this room and the reception area *clean*. I mean fuckin' *spotless*. Volpe wants the place immaculate. *Always!*"

"Yeah, I noticed that. Good to know," Jessica responded obediently.

"And there's no smoking allowed," Debbie threw in.

Of all the things Jessica thought would be more important about what to *do* and *not do* in such a place, she chuckled as she answered, "No problem. I don't smoke."

It was a few minutes before two o'clock when Debbie and Jessica finally stepped into the reception area through the door to the treatment rooms. Patricia, still on the sofa sketching in her pad, couldn't help overhearing her co-worker tell the new employee, "You'll need to remember all the girls' names."

Though Jessica was thinking it, Patricia jokingly yelled out, "Yeah! Just like *you* do!" which caused the three of them to laugh.

With interest, Patricia watched the banter between Debbie's rough edge and Jessica's innocence and naivete.

"There's a roster of names and their schedules in the desk somewhere. You'll figure it out." Once again, Debbie remembered something important. "And we each have rules. I know one girl, Betty Jean, she won't do amputees."

Jessica's eyebrows shot up as she asked, "Get a lot of those?"

"Not a lot, but we *do* get some wounded soldiers once in a while," Patricia answered, sympathetically. "When they *do* come in, and if I get them, I treat them extra special."

Debbie resumed the list of who does-and-doesn't do what.

"You'll need to talk to each therapist to find out their quirks. A couple of 'em won't do Persians, you know, Iranians. There's a shitload of 'em around here, too. It's funny, 'cause the Persian Empire ended seventeen-hundred-fucking-years ago. My family was from Denmark, but we don't go around saying we're Vikings, for Christsake." Jessica was briefly impressed with Debbie's knowledge of world history as she went on. "A couple of girls don't do women…and I don't--"

"Women? Customers? You have women come here?" Jessica blurted.

With a smile, Patricia erotically answered, "This isn't your everyday massage parlor, honey."

"Who did you think the women's locker room was for? Think *we're* the only ones taking showers between clients?" Debbie asked with a laugh.

Jessica could only give a stunned look. She was learning a *lot* about Diamond Jim's clientele, and she hadn't even sat her "cute little ass" behind the big oak desk yet.

"Oh…and talking about showers, I don't do them," Debbie continued.

Confused, Jessica asked, "Showers? You mean you won't take a shower with someone?"

The two therapists giggled as Debbie replied, "No. You know… where the guy wants you to piss on them."

Jessica's facial reaction made it obvious she had never heard of such a thing.

"Anyway," Debbie said, "I don't do that."

Patricia sarcastically blurted out, "Ahhh, a girl with standards."

Again, all three busted out laughing.

Debbie gave Jessica an odd look and asked, "You've never had a guy you dated ask for that? Where have you been?"

The doorbell rang.

Jessica and Debbie went behind the desk, checked the video monitor, then the new employee buzzed in another therapist and the two locker room attendants before finally responding to Debbie's question by admitting, "Uh…until several months ago…" the words were hard to get out, but she pushed herself to say them. "I was married. I mean, I'm *still* married…but I'm separated. He said he wanted more fun in his life and that I was plain and boring." With a chuckle she added, "I guess I should have pissed on him." The three of them again laughed, then she changed the subject. "How, uh…where do they get this number? A website?"

"There's no website," the artist answered. "It's mostly longtime clients and referrals."

Again, Debbie interjected her knowledge of statistics, "And we never run at less than eighty-three percent capacity usually from six o'clock to closing."

Jessica was awed.

It was nearly 3:20PM.

Patricia, Debbie and four of the therapists were already in their treatment rooms. Three were with clients, and three were waiting to be called to fetch clients who were currently in the shower, steam room or sauna. Two middle aged men sat at the small oak table, each enjoying a cocktail made by the 24-year-old kimono clad bartender as they waited for their appointment to start. However, by the look of them and their familiarity with Diamond Jim's… they were in no rush.

With the alarm fob next to her, Jessica sat at the desk reading the roster of names, their schedules and the information she was required to complete in "the book" for each appointment. She was also watching what was going on around her…though she held back any sign of how shocked at herself she was for even being *in* such a place, and also her surprise of how professionally and skillfully it was being operated. The five clients who had arrived within the last hour were well-dressed, polite and professional.

The phone rang. It was Jessica's first call. Picking up the receiver and the script…she took a deep breath and gave it her best shot.

"Hi, Diamond Jim's!" she attempted to cheerfully say. She listened to the caller, then answered, "Yes, your friend was right," then listened again and replied, "That's the price for the first hour. Would you like to make an appointment?"

CLICK!

She looked at the receiver, said, "Guess not" and hung up.

The door leading from the treatment rooms opened and "Nurse Debbie" emerged. Two minutes later a man in his early 60s, wearing a tailored suit and carrying a medical bag emerged from the locker room door…looking spent.

As she walked him toward the receptionist's desk, Debbie asked, "Same time next week, Doc?"

He grinned, nodded, winked and handed Jessica an envelope with Debbie's name on it.

After both women smiled and thanked him, Debbie led him out the front door and shut it.

Jessica heard the electronic lock…and smiled at its sound. She opened the envelope, removed five one-hundred dollar bills, logged it in the book under Debbie's tips and replaced the cash into the envelope.

Debbie returned to the desk and told Jessica, "He's really a doctor and just loves his bag of tricks."

With more than a little uncertainty, Jessica said, "I just hope I have the kind of voice that'll make the callers come in."

Debbie gave a friendly grin and said, "It's easy. Just the fact that they called means they're interested in coming here in the first place. They just need you to seal the deal. Make your voice more inviting…sensual. You know how to do that, don't you?"

Jessica chuckled and replied, "I'm not sure. It's been a long time."

"Look at it this way, Jessie, the more clients…the more money," said Debbie. Her words were certainly a motivating factor…though Jessica despised being call "Jessie."

The phone rang.

"Give it a shot," Debbie said. "I have to get out of this outfit and get ready for my next client."

With her best bubbly and sensual voice, Jessica picked up the receiver, looked at the script and gave it her best shot.

"Hi, Diamond Jim's!"

She listened to the caller, then in a low sexy tone she replied, "As you know, we offer a very sensual, full body-to-body rubdown." She listened again, smiled and asked, "Ah, you *have?* Do you have a special lady?" As she listened, she picked up the roster and quickly replied, "Yes, Tia *is* here today and has a few openings." Jessica stopped dead, realized what she said and laughed out loud. Containing herself, she perused the schedule and asked, "Is five-thirty good for you?"

CHAPTER 5
For Zat You Get A Time Dot's Vunderbar, Shatzi.
Very Vunderbar

Like Jessica was previously told, most of the calls came from Diamond Jim's regulars who didn't require 'the pitch.' She also learned how to tell the difference between them and those who had yet to walk in the door for the first time. It didn't take long before she began referring to the script less and less, while the schedule filled up more and more. When she wasn't answering the phone, writing the client's and therapist's details in the book, filling the schedule, eyeing the fob and security screens, or dropping cash and credit card receipts into the vault...she was looking at her leather folio filled with sheet music.

Jessica continued to practice her piano every morning, plus she'd read songbooks and sheet music from the folio like others would read magazines and novels. And yet, she was only making $120 a week teaching students during her days off.

Music and her piano were the only remaining loves of Jessica's life.

It was Jessica's fourth day, and all was going well. Since it was a Saturday, all eight rooms had therapists working. She brought CDs from home that ranged from piano concertos to schmaltzy lounge tunes...and as they played, she'd be reading music charts and bobbing her head to their tempos.

Neither the clients nor the therapists complained, which made her happy.

And as always, the alarm fob was never out of reach.

It was a little after 8:30PM when Ingrid entered the reception area through the hallway door. She was in her early 30s and had a bad blonde dye-job, a German accent and was dressed in a tight blouse and skirt with the tops of her breasts sticking out. Ingrid was not the classiest of the ladies who worked at Diamond Jim's, nor was she well-liked by her co-workers. Approaching Jessica's desk, she pulled out a vaporizer, took a long hit off of it and exhaled a cloud of sweet-smelling smoke.

Before she was able to say anything to the receptionist, the phone rang.

As Ingrid watched, Jessica answered, "Hi, Diamond Jim's!"

After listening for a few seconds, Jessica responded with, "Yes, we *do* know him, and it's nice that he recommended us. Let me explain the details. We offer a very sensual, body-to-body rubdown." The caller asked a question, to which Jessica replied, "Yes, two-hundred-and-fifty for the first--" The caller interrupted, causing her to quickly retort, "I'm sorry, but that's our price."

Ingrid reached across the desk, grabbed the handset from the unsuspecting Jessica and told the caller, "For zat you get a time dot's vunderbar, shatzi. *Very* vunderbar. And I promise…you'll love it. Vhat's your name, honey?" She listened. "Hi, Greg, I'm Ingrid! So, I'll see you in twenty minutes, ja? You know zee address?" She made sure he had it right, then said, "Ve can talk about zee extras ven you get here." He agreed. "Good. Auf wiedersehen."

The therapist handed the phone to Jessica, who hung it up and wrote "Greg" under Ingrid's name in the logbook and on the schedule.

"I thought we had to be careful about what we say on the phone?" the receptionist asked.

"I don't come here to vaste time," the German answered. "I get zem in, turn zem on, get zem off, get ze gratuity and get zem out. Your job is to get zem through zat door so I can make zat happen. *You* say vatever zey need to hear so zey come in…and *I'll* take it from zhere."

Ingrid took another long hit off the vaporizer, let out a pungent cloud, then reached into her purse, took out a tube of lipstick and put on too much. Way too much.

Not being impressed with this particular therapist, and knowing they were never going to be friends, Jessica asked, "Want to tell me what you're doing in there?" as she pointed to the door leading to the treatment rooms.

"Zat depends on how much zey pay, sveetheart. You think we get zhose kinds of tips from rubbing lotion on zheir backs?" she countered, then raised her voice and belted out, "Vake up! I can make a guy come two minutes after he gets hard."

Ingrid had said it so loud that besides Jessica, the bartender *also* let out a laugh.

"Zey *love* having baby oil dripped on zheir cocks," Ingrid continued with a chuckle. "Zey pay for an hour, but I can get zem in-and-out in half that…*vit* a tip! I don't like lookin' at zem much longer zan zat."

Stunned at what she was hearing and how candid Ingrid was being, Jessica asked, "What got you *into* this business?"

Without taking more than a second to contemplate the answer, Ingrid replied, "I love ze sex…and I love ze money. Just not in zat order."

The receptionist smiled, but kept her thoughts to herself.

"And now…I must get ready for ze *Greg*."

The receptionist smiled even more once this one particular therapist walked away.

It was 11:43PM by the time Jessica opened the door to her Chatsworth apartment. She went inside, locked the door, dropped her purse and keys on the dining room table, stripped naked and fell onto her bed. Within minutes she was asleep.

That was when the house phone rang.

Jessica thought she was dreaming.

It wasn't until the fourth ring that she woke up enough to throw her arm toward the night table to pick up the extension's receiver, then with her face pressed into a pillow, she muttered the almost incomprehensible words, "Hi, Diamond Ji--"

Realizing where she was, "*Shit!*" was the next word out of her mouth.

Coming to her senses, she asked, "Yeah?"

"*You're asleep? Now?* It's only midnight and the first Saturday in three months I'm not playin'!" belted out Suzanne. "Get your ass outta bed and meet me at The Zone. We'll celebrate."

"Celebrate *what?*" Jessica groggily asked.

"Your first week! How was it?"

"I'm drained, Suz. I can *not* believe I'm even working there. It's not as innocent as you made it sound."

"So, how much did you make?" Suzanne asked.

Jessica was silent.

"Jess?" Suzanne pressed.

"How did *you* know I got paid tonight?"

"I took a shot. So?"

"Seventeen-hundred-and-eighty-eight dollars."

In a stall of The Zone's ladies room, Suzanne was sitting on the toilet with her cell phone to her ear. Her free hand went into her purse, then took out a small vial of white powder and twisted the top off as she responded, "Get the fuck outta here. Jess! You *never* made that kind-a cash playing at Valentina's! C'mon...the first three shots are on you!" She put the vial to her nostril and quietly took a hit.

Jessica, whose face was still in her pillow, said, "No. Not tonight. Tomorrow. Coffee."

"Look, Jess...I know this job's not *you*. But making that kind of cash every week? You'll have your life in order before you know it."

Jessica's eyes opened slightly to respond, "Suz...you know I love you, but I gotta get some sleep. We'll talk about it tomorrow. G'night." Then she remembered something. "Oh! You still there?"

"Yeah."

"Suzanne…thank you. Thanks for being there for me. Thanks for helping."

"I'm your friend, Jess. I'll *always* be there for you. Now…get to sleep."

Jessica fumbled the phone, hung up and closed her eyes.

CHAPTER 6
What's *Your* Mission?

It may have been the 4th of July, 2015, outside Diamond Jim's door, but inside it was business as usual and just another Saturday. Jessica had done an outstanding job of keeping the schedule and treatment rooms filled. It was the end of her third week as an employee, and though she had mixed thoughts about the industry she found herself a part of, there were still no jobs listed or being offered for a lounge or restaurant pianist.

She had now been taking home nearly eighteen-hundred dollars a week *after* taxes, which not only helped with her unpaid bills and divorce attorney, but having such an income for a job she felt held no 'corporate responsibilities' other than being honest with the boss's money, brought Jessica peace of mind, which allowed her to sleep better.

By this point, Jessica had been legally separated for a little over fifteen months and her attorney had assured her they would go to court to finalize the divorce as soon as they had reached the eighteen month anniversary of the papers being signed and filed.

It was 7:15PM. Three men, unfamiliar to one another, found a few common things to joke about as the bartender brought their assorted drinks to the table in the reception area. An instrumental version of "*Days Of Wine And* Roses" played through the speakers. It was a favorite of Jessica's and had been in 'high rotation' on the 5-disc CD player.

Darryl sat on a sofa reading a magazine.

Jessica was at her desk with the music folio open to a manuscript of charts. The fob rested next to the desk phone.

Darryl's cell phone buzzed. Eyeing the text message, he stood, walked into the office, then shut and locked the door.

Once inside, he flipped a small switch behind the camera, which froze the video image on the security screen that was visible on Jessica's monitor. Opening the cabinet, he knelt in front of the bottom compartment, opened the wooden door and tapped in the safe's code. As soon as it unlocked, he reached in and collected the cash and credit card receipts, then very neatly folded and tucked them into the inside pockets of his sport jacket.

Darryl efficiently closed the safe, shut the wooden cabinet doors and flipped the switch on the security camera to reinstate the live image before returning to the reception area.

Once there, he walked directly to the desk and told Jessica, "Listen…"

She took her eyes from the sheet music and looked up.

"I want you to know something," he continued. "When I come back later with the pay envelopes," he proudly grinned, "You're getting a five-hundred dollar bonus this week for doing a good job. You're putting everything in the book, you're bringing in new clients, you're keeping your desk and the office clean, the music you brought in don't suck…and even *the ladies* like you. It pays to have someone like you working here."

Before she could respond, he said, "I gotta go. Hold down the fort."

As he left, the three men in the reception area were informed their therapists were ready. Each was led into the locker room by the bartender, to whom a sizeable tip was given.

To a degree, Jessica enjoyed having the next three days off.

She spent Sunday afternoon at a gourmet barbeque with Charlie at the Woodland Hills home of Constance, her friends from Valentina's.

Monday turned into a funk once Jessica looked at the file containing her divorce paperwork to see that it was a year since Leon had moved away. Around four o'clock she decided to get out of the apartment and take one of the scenic drives to Malibu. Once her feet touched the sand, she walked along the shoreline until six-thirty, then enjoyed a peaceful and private dinner sitting along the railing at Geoffrey's on the Pacific Coast Highway.

Tuesday was her day with the sticky-fingered kids playing their unpracticed lessons on her baby grand…and again, around four o'clock, she took a different scenic route to Malibu, walked an alternate shoreline, and again dined along the railing at Geoffrey's, though ordered a different entrée.

Each evening, as she quietly ate her meals overlooking the Pacific, she recalled different eras and aspects of her thirty-two years…and how much had changed during the last fourteen months.

Wednesday, July 8th would be another day Jessica would remember for the rest of her life.

Outside it was cloudy and 75 degrees at 2:30PM, but inside, as the receptionist had learned, it was always 'business as usual' in Diamond Jim's.

By now, Jessica had the rap down…right down to the closing.

"…that includes cocktails, steam and sauna rooms, and a *very* sensual body-to-body rubdown," she pleasantly spoke into the phone. "What's your name, honey?" She listened, then continued. "Well, Peter, if you'd like to make an appointment…I'm sure you'll find out."

She smiled to herself, wrote "Peter" in the book, then said, "Good. See you in an hour," and returned the receiver to its base.

Though he appeared to be reading a Time magazine, Darryl was watching and listening from his spot on one of the sofas.

"A busy day ahead?" he asked.

"Well, there's the normal number of clients booked, but I'm a little concerned because Ingrid hasn't shown up yet, and she hasn't called. I called her cell but got her voicemail. I left a message, but no call back yet."

"Maybe she's stuck in traffic or somewhere in a canyon with no signal. If you don't hear from her by three, call someone off the roster and get 'em in here."

Darryl's cell phone rang. Answering it before the second ring, he listened to the caller and responded, "Yes, sir," then hung up. He stood and said to Jessica, "You're doin' fine, girl. Just keep it up and hold down the fort. You need anything, call me."

She nodded as he headed for the door.

Jessica listened to the lock after he stepped outside and watched him on the security camera as he walked to his car. When Ingrid hadn't shown by three o'clock, she called four therapists, but none answered. She left messages letting them know that the first to call back could have the bookings.

At 3:22PM, the door from the treatment rooms opened and out walked Patricia. A moment later the locker room door opened and out stepped a stunning, corporate-attired woman in her late 40s…and she was smiling. *Happily* smiling. As Patricia led her to the receptionist's desk, the therapist was smiling, too.

Handing a credit card to Jessica, the woman said, "Please give my friend Patricia six-hundred dollars."

Jessica put the chip end of the card into the phone, tapped the appropriate amount into the keyboard and let technology do the rest. The woman keyed in her code, the receipts were printed…and the transaction was complete.

As Patricia led her client to the door, Jessica looked at the only woman in Diamond Jim's she felt a friendship toward, and grinned at the fact that her friend had just been with a woman, something Jessica felt she could never do.

Just like peeing on a man.

After the door electronically locked, Patricia approached the desk. Jessica took the large sketchpad from under the leather music folio and handed it to her. As Patricia sat on one of the sofas, Jessica gave her the bad news.

"You know that ninety-minute window you thought you had that was to start right now?"

"Yeah?" replied Patricia suspiciously as she opened the pad's cover to work on her most recent piece.

"A new client. Peter. He'll be here in about ten minutes…and you're the only one free. Sorry. Not having Ingrid here screwed up the schedule. I made a few calls, but no one's called back yet."

As Patricia began to draw, she said, "No problem. I still have time to clean up while he hits the locker room. That reminds me… tomorrow's my birthday, so don't make any plans for after work. You and me need a night out and away from this place. What do you think of Don Cuco in Simi Valley for dinner and drinks?"

Having never been there, and just happy to be asked to go out, Jessica's answer was easy.

"Sure!" she replied while craning her neck to see what Patricia was sketching.

"It's an assignment," the artist happily told her. "One more semester and I'll have my B.A. in Art."

Patricia turned the pad, showing a rough sketch of a female figure wearing a majestic blue evening gown covered in sequins that also revealed a red bustier, garter and stockings. There was the outline of a head, but no face.

Jessica nodded, impressed by her friend's talent, and asked, "What the hell are you doing *here?*"

Patricia replied with a laugh, "Even with partial scholarships and grants, a degree doesn't come easy. Not as easy as these guys do," which made them *both* laugh. "Show me another job where I can work three days a week and make two grand or more, get my taxes paid, some health insurance…and I'm in."

Patricia kept sketching as their conversation went on.

"Good point," Jessica said, "But doesn't it bother you to be touching these guys..." Then she recalled who just left a six-hundred dollar tip, and threw in, "...and women?"

The artist stopped sketching, looked at Jessica with sincerity and honesty, and replied, "You know, once you do it and get paid for it...paid *well* for it...it becomes as mindless as brushing your teeth. You realize you're just in it for the cash...and that's it."

Jessica's face showed she wasn't sold on it.

"I'll tell you, Jessica, when we met, I knew you didn't belong here. *I don't* either...but I'm on a mission and I knew what I was getting myself into when I took this job. This place isn't for you. You should get out and find a *real* job...a more suitable job. Find a job playing your piano. I know it's a bitch, and I know you've got a lot going on. We've talked a lot about it over the last couple of weeks and I've been watching you. You're smart. You'll get back on your feet. You just have to find out what your mission is, that's all." Sounding confident and trying to be reassuring, Patricia said, "Trust me on that, Jess."

Jessica, both curious and interested, asked, "What's *your* mission?"

Without hesitation, Patricia responded, "I know *what* I want and where I want it *to be*. Working here is just a means to that end. Once I finish school--"

Just then, the doorbell rang.

Jessica turned to the video screen to see the innocent-looking, well-dressed, 27-year-old Peter waiting to be buzzed in, and said, "Shit. He's a little early."

Patricia calmly closed the sketchpad, walked to the desk, handed the pad to Jessica and asked, "What's his name again?"

"Peter."

As Patricia swayed her way to the door, Jessica returned her gaze to the folio of charts.

Pulling the door open, Patricia sensually said with a smile, "You must be Peter!" She offered her hand before he could respond, "Come on in and make yourself comfortable."

Patricia took his arm as they walked to the receptionist's desk and asked, "Have you ever been here before, Peter?"

He shyly grinned and answered, "No, never. A couple of my friends have been coming here for a while. One of 'em for a couple of years. You may know him. Morley--"

Smiling at his innocence, Patricia cut him off.

"We don't need to know who, honey. Privacy is the first rule of what we sell here. The fact that you had our phone number means someone who's enjoyed our therapists recommended you."

Her tone and charm seemed to calm him a bit.

At the desk, Patricia said, "This is Jess. Take care of business with her, then relax out here and have a drink, if you'd like. When you're ready, you'll be shown to the locker room where we have steam and sauna rooms, and of course, showers. When you're ready, the attendant will let me know. Okay?"

Astounded by the efficiency and amenities, the newbie stammered, "Sure. Thanks."

Peter watched Patricia sensuously sway across the reception area to the therapists' door as he removed $260 in new twenties from his wallet and handed them to Jessica.

"Let me guess. You hit the cash machine before you got here?" she joked.

He smiled and nodded as she handed him a ten-dollar bill, placed his payment in the drawer and suggested he have the pretty Asian bartender make him a drink to relax.

It took Peter less than ten minutes to consume his Bacardi and Coke, after which the bartender led him into the locker room.

Jessica watched it all with a smile.

Once inside, the attendant provided Peter a locker key, rubber sandals and two towels before giving him a tour of the other amenities.

Jessica's smile continued as the phone rang. She put the receiver to the side of her head and happily chimed, "Hi, Diamond Jim's!"

With her other hand she turned a page in the folio and scanned a chart.

The deep, cool, masculine voice that came through the phone made Jessica divert her eyes from the music.

"It's Volpe."

Taken by surprise, all she could say was, "Excuse me?"

"It's Volpe. Are you *deaf?*"

Jessica was dismayed at his comeback.

He continued, "Ah! You're the new girl."

Out of character, Jessica sarcastically replied, "Three weeks, actually. Not exactly new."

Not listening to what she was saying, he asked, "How we doin'?"

Jessica eyed the schedule and replied, "Well, we've only been open an hour-and-a-half, and I have six rooms booked pretty much throughout the day. But one of the girls didn't show--"

Volpe interrupted and said, "Oh, Ingrid...I fired her. She was a pig. She gets the clients out too fast and she says too much on the phone. You want her shift?"

Trying to decide between being insulted and wanting to laugh, Jessica replied, "You know I'm not a masseuse, right?"

Indifferently, he again responded as if not hearing her, "Check the phone list and get someone in there to take her place."

"Already done. Just waiting for a call back."

"Yeah, that's right. Darryl said you were the smart one. You know, if you need anything..."

They simultaneously said, "Call Darryl."

She laughed. He showed no humor in his response of, "And don't forget...keep the place clean. It makes me sick when it's dirty. Capisi?"

Before she could utter another sound, he coolly said, "Ciao, bella," then hung up.

She looked at the receiver and sarcastically returned with, "Nice talking to you, too. *Ciao.*"

Hanging up the receiver, Jessica shook her head and began to straighten up her desk...then stopped to talk to herself.

"What the hell am I doing in this place? Oh, that's right…the *money*." Getting serious, she muttered, "Patricia's right. I gotta get out of here."

CHAPTER 7
Anger Clouds Your Path To Clarity And It Pains Your Heart

Over the next hour, male and female clients came and went. Each stopped at the desk when they arrived and again when they departed. And each time, there was a smile on their face.

Jessica made sure every dollar and credit card receipt that passed through her hands were correctly logged into the book, then deposited into the safe.

On the first trip into the office after Volpe's call, Jessica scanned the therapists' certificates on the wall to see Ingrid Schüttel's had been removed.

Returning to her large oak desk, the frustrated pianist admired Patricia's sketchpad and enjoyed the music emanating from the reception area speakers.

At exactly 4:30PM, Peter stepped out of the locker room door and approached the desk. Patricia was already sitting on the sofa across from Jessica. The young man's eyes glazed with happiness and satisfaction when Patricia rose to stand next to him as he happily handed Jessica the tip envelope, then the therapist led him to the front door.

As Patricia closed the door behind him, a hand gently pushed it open and a friendly male voice said, "Hi! I have a four-fifteen appointment, and I'm a little late. Sorry."

"Your name?" she asked.

"Tommy. I made an appointment last Friday." He smiled at the attractive therapist before him and said, "I've been here before."

Patricia held up a finger for him to wait, closed the door and turned to Jessica.

"You have a Tommy at four-fifteen?"

Jessica looked at the schedule, laughed and said, "Yeah…he was originally on Ingrid's list."

Patricia opened the wooden door and cooed, "Come on in, Tommy."

As the good-looking, well-dressed man in his late 40s stepped in, she observed a noticeable limp on his left side. Offering her arm, she asked, "So, you've been here before?"

"About five or six weeks ago…with a blonde. German, I think."

"That was Ingrid. She's not working today." The therapist cocked her head and sensuously asked, "I'm Patricia. Will I do?"

Tommy smiled and nodded.

Before taking a few steps, the doorbell rang *again*…causing Patricia to glance at Jessica for some kind of verification of who it could be.

The receptionist said, "It's probably Tia. But she said she couldn't get here until five." Looking at the video screen, she exclaimed, "Nope. It's a short, stocky, well-dressed Asian man wearing round glasses. Must be a client showing up early."

"Oh, no," Patricia said under her breath. She politely excused herself from Tommy and told him to, "See the cute lady behind the desk."

Upon reaching Jessica, he handed her three one-hundred dollar bills.

She opened the drawer, took out a $50 bill, handed it to him as she smiled and said, "C'mon, let's get you to the locker room so you can get comfortable."

He replied softly, "If you don't mind, because of my leg, I'd rather not deal with the locker room…" his face saddened, "…and people." He forced a smile as he continued, "I took a shower just before I came here. I'm nice and clean, honest." The two of them chuckled. "I just feel odd, that's all. Is it okay? Ingrid didn't have a problem with it the last time I was here."

"I understand. Just let me check with Patricia first. Why don't you have a seat and a drink if you'd like. She should be back in a minute."

"I'll take the seat. No need for the drink," he said as he limped to the small oak table and sat down.

At the same time, Patricia had opened the door to find one of her regular clients and said with surprise, "*Mr. Watanabe!* What are you doing here? You don't have an appointment and I have someone ready to get on the table."

"Ah! Miss Pat," he said in a thick Japanese accent, "Apologies for unannounced arrival. I wish to see you for only short time."

She led Mr. Watanabe inside, then directly to Jessica's desk and asked her, "What kind of time do I have? Is anyone free to take Tommy?"

Jessica scanned the schedule and answered, "You have a short break after Tommy." She then pointed to Tommy seated at the table. "He's, uh, he's ready to get in the treatment room right now."

"No shower?" the therapist inquisitively asked.

"Talk to him," was Jessica's response.

Patricia turned and asked Mr. Watanabe, "Can you come back later?"

"No need," he answered. "For you I wait, Miss Pat."

The therapist and receptionist looked at one another and shrugged.

He bowed to the two women and they returned the gesture.

Patricia led him to one of the sofas, saying, "Make yourself comfortable, Mr. Watanabe. I'll be back to get you as soon as I can." Then she turned to Jessica and said, "Hon, this is Mr. Watanabe... an absolute gentleman. Keep him company for a little while, will you?"

Jessica smiled at him.

Mr. Watanabe smiled back as he sat.

Patricia returned to Tommy. They quietly spoke for a moment, then she nodded, opened the door and led him down the hallway to her treatment room.

Meanwhile, Jessica wrote Tommy's therapist and payment details into the book, then looked at Mr. Watanabe as he contentedly, quietly and politely waited.

"Can I get you anything, Mr. Watanabe? Water? A drink? A magazine? It's going to be a while."

"No, thank you. Very nice to offer. I wait for Miss Pat," he returned.

Jessica nodded, then went back to viewing the charts within the folio and listening to the music.

Every so often a contented client would exit the locker room and stop at Jessica's desk to complete their transaction, but for the most part, things quieted down during the dinner hour. As promised, Tia arrived just before five o'clock. At ten-after-five Jessica figured it would be a good time to take care of some personal business… so she picked up the desk phone, dialed and waited for an answer.

"Lois Hansen, please. It's Jessica." Listening for a couple of seconds, she then replied, "Yes. She left a message on my home phone asking me to call." Jessica cordially smiled again at Mr. Watanabe as she was put on hold. He respectfully smiled back. Hearing her divorce attorney's voice, Jessica said, "Hi, Lois. What's up?"

As she listened, her face turned pale and her eyes widened.

The always-calm Jessica yelled into the receiver, "That *bastard!*"

Watanabe raised his eyebrows and watched her.

With rage in her voice, she barked, "*No! No way!* You tell that son-of-a-bitch the only way he'll get my piano is over my *dead-fucking-body!*"

With shock and embarrassment on her face, Jessica lowered the phone and thought about what she had just said to her attorney. "Fuck" was not a word Jessica was known to use.

The door to the treatment rooms burst open as Patricia, "Nurse Debbie" and Tia rushed into the reception area. They were quickly joined by the bartender.

Jessica held up the phone, cupped her hand over the mouthpiece, looked at the women and angrily said, "My attorney."

They each sympathetically shook their heads. Patricia put an index finger to her lips, letting Jessica know she needed to be quiet, then the therapists and bartender returned to their jobs.

Jessica lowered her volume and returned to the call...but with *just* as much anger.

"*Of course* you can take that as a '*No!*'" Her eyes filled with tears as she tried to control herself. "You call his lawyer and tell that sonofabitch he's out of his mind." As Jessica slammed down the receiver, she angrily glared at Mr. Watanabe.

A man.

He politely leaned toward her and sympathetically asked, "Would you like water?"

With as much composure as she could muster, Jessica looked down at the desk and shook her head.

"Would you like to use unfortunate situation to advantage?" he posed.

Jessica, confused, raised her head.

"Huh? What are you talking about?"

"Your anger. Would you like to prosper from your anger?" he inoffensively queried.

With an even mixture of resentment and sarcasm in her voice, Jessica asked, "How? Meditate? No."

"Slap me," he calmly replied.

"Excuse me?"

"Slap me," he repeated just as calmly the second time.

"Why?"

"I have my reasons...as in life, you have yours."

"You want me to slap you?"

"And I will give you four hundred dollar...for one minute."

"You're kidding?"

The Asian man slowly shook his head, took a Salvatore Ferragamo billfold from his jacket, produced four $100 bills and removed his glasses.

"I can't," Jessica said from deep within her.

"You are very angry at someone. Anger clouds your path to clarity and it pains your heart. You must not hold anger within. You must use it. You must release it, or...it will devour you." He gave a pleasant grin and continued, "Imagine, for only moment, I am person who angers you."

Jessica, with rage in her eyes, looked at the phone. As the bartender watched, Jessica stood from behind the desk, walked to the seated Watanabe, pulled her right arm back, opened her hand and *whacked* his face.

He smiled.

The bartender smiled.

Jessica was shocked at what she did, and in her loudest voice cried out, "Oh my god! *I'm so sorry!*"

Still smiling, he responded, "Again, please."

Unsure of what to say, she stuttered, "But...but..."

"Call to lawyer cost one-hundred dollar, maybe more."

She raised her left arm and slapped him *hard*.

Watanabe smiled.

She was momentarily grateful he didn't ask her to pee on him.

Once again, the door to the treatment rooms opened. Patricia, about thirty-five minutes into Tommy's massage, bolted in.

"What the hell was *that?*" Patricia asked as she saw Mr. Watanabe sitting, grinning, with cash in his hand. Jessica was standing in front of him with her stinging open palms. She turned to Patricia, not sure how to explain what she had just done, because she didn't understand it herself.

Patricia looked at the bartender, who motioned that all was well. Understanding, the therapist returned her eyes to Jessica, and with a *big* grin, said, "*You're* going to take care of him? Good for you. Thanks. But you gotta keep it down, honey." Then she winked at Jessica and returned to work.

"One full minute. Continue please," implored Mr. Watanabe. "Someone wants your piano. Are you going to give it to him?"

Jessica pulled her right arm back and let another slap *wail*.

"That might be what he *wants*," she furiously-but-softly growled. "But it's not what he's gonna…"

She slapped Watanabe again.

"…*get!*"

The pianist continued to smack and backhand him with musical timing as she repeated in a low, angry voice, "Who the hell do you think you are?" three or four times.

While Mr. Watanabe was at the beginning of his offer to Jessica, relaxing music was playing in Patricia's elegantly decorated treatment room. Tommy, with his eyes closed, had been face-down on the table for about thirty-five minutes. His mid-section was covered by a warm towel, and his clothes neatly hung from hangers on the door. Patricia was professionally massaging and kneading the man's muscles, and had just finished working on the ball of his left foot.

It was then that she heard Jessica on the phone yelling at her attorney.

Excusing herself in the most professional manner, Patricia told Tommy, "I'd like you to slowly turn over and cover yourself with the towel. I'll be right back."

As she walked out of the room, he did as he was told, and as promised, Patricia returned less than two minutes later.

She stood behind Tommy's head and professionally massaged and manipulated his neck and shoulders. A moment later she heard Jessica yell *again*…causing the masseuse to excuse herself *again*.

"I'm sorry, Tommy," she explained, "The girl out there is pretty new and I have to make sure everything's okay. I'll make it up to you as soon as I get back." she said with a giggle.

He responded with a thumbs up as she went back to the reception area to find that "the new girl" would be taking care of her Japanese client.

Returning to her room and unseen by Tommy, Patricia undid the top two buttons of her blouse as she took her time expertly kneading the muscles of the fit man. While working on his legs, she eyed two round scars on the front of his left leg that she recognized as bullet wounds. She eventually massaged her way to his shoulders, neck and the top of his head.

Seeing an obvious bump under Tommy's towel, she opened two more shirt buttons allowing her breasts to be exposed and sway above him as she reached over his head to massage his chest...and he saw them.

Nothing was said for a long moment as each enjoyed what was happening, then Patricia offered, "I can take care of that for you, if you'd like."

With a smile, Tommy happily asked, "How much?"

Jessica stood in front of Mr. Watanabe, stunned at herself and at his red and swollen face.

Mindful of the volume of her voice, she cried, "Oh my god, Mr. Watanabe! Look what I've done to you! I'm *so* sorry."

Not changing his expression, he serenely replied, "Continue please."

"No...I can't. It's wrong."

Mr. Watanabe raised his hand with the cash.

She looked at it. Her eyes filled with *more* tears.

"Wrong? So is taking piano," he tranquilly said.

The bartender's eyes were focused on Jessica's debut performance, so neither she, Jessica nor Mr. Watanabe noticed the treatment room door open as Patricia and Tommy entered the reception area.

Detective Tom "Tommy" Brogan was dressed. Patricia's shirt was open with her breasts exposed and her hands were behind her back.

Jessica took a deep breath, raised her hand and again repeatedly slapped Mr. Watanabe's face and said in a low guttural voice, "I *loved* you! I *trusted* you! I'll *never* let you take it!" Then she slapped him again. "*Never!*"

She stopped her open-handed assault, collected herself, then wiped away her tears.

Watanabe leaned back into the sofa…as if sexually spent. He respectfully bowed his head, held the money toward Jessica and appreciatively said, "Thank you. That was most…pleasurable."

Jessica, not believing what she had done, ashamedly took the money.

As Mr. Watanabe was putting on his glasses, Tommy yelled for all to hear, "*Nice job!* I thought I was walkin' into a remake of Chinatown."

No one got the referenced connection.

Jessica turned to see Detective Brogan holding up his badge.

She looked at Patricia, who turned to reveal she had been handcuffed.

Jessica and Watanabe were speechless.

At that moment, a battering ram crashed through the locked wooden front door.

The bartender, Jessica, Mr. Watanabe and Patricia were startled as six detectives stormed inside with their guns drawn.

Instinctively, Jessica reached for the fob atop the desk. Two detectives, just as instinctively, pointed their pistols at her and a third brought the butt of his gun down onto the fob, smashing it… an inch away from the leather music folio and Patricia's sketchpad.

Brogan pointed to four of the detectives and said, "There's a few more in the back rooms."

As the detectives entered the treatment room door, Brogan looked at Jessica and chuckled, "Prostitution's one thing. But an S&M shop, *too?* Interesting. Funny…you don't look the type." He looked at Mr. Watanabe and ordered a detective to get the usual information and send him on his way.

Brogan led Jessica to a wall, then frisked her.

She was humiliated.

She pressed her head against the wall…angry at herself…and angry at the world.

"I only answer the phone," Jessica irately told Brogan.

"Yeah," he sarcastically replied. "That's *exactly* what it looked like you were doing."

"Quiet, honey," Patricia said to the nervous Jessica.

"Good advice," replied Brogan, then, as he put handcuffs on Jessica, he continued with, "But let me put it another way. You have the right to remain silent. Anything you say can and will be used against you…"

The four detectives returned with five handcuffed ladies in various outfits and stages of undress, and an equal number of men with towels around their waists. Two of the therapists were Debbie and Tia.

After getting Mr. Watanabe's identification and story, the detective dismissed him by sarcastically saying, "Take a hike, homeboy." It took a second before the Asian man got it, but once he did, he bowed his head and bolted.

CHAPTER 8
So I Was Pissed Off And This Guy Said, "Slap Me"

The five customers were each processed, fined $200 and released shortly after being taken into custody.

By eight o'clock on Wednesday night, July 8th, 2015…Jessica Ross Farber had been handcuffed, formally arrested, read her Miranda Rights, fingerprinted, had mug shots taken and spent more than an hour alone in a cell within the Malibu/Lost Hills Sheriff's Station on Agoura Road in Agoura.

Detective Tom Brogan sat in his office processing the required paperwork detailing the bust and subsequent arrests, and was also mentally preparing questions for his interrogation of Jessica.

Not having a criminal attorney to defend her for the crimes she was being accused of, Jessica accepted the use of a court appointed public defender to be present during her questioning. She asked to be represented by a female and was told, "Sure," by one of the handful of detectives processing the accumulated documents in her case file.

Spending about thirty minutes with Nicholas Barker, the early 40s non-female court appointed lawyer, the frustrated and handcuffed Jessica explained *twice* about how and when she got the job, what her function was, and that she had no knowledge about the owner, only that everyone who worked there, "…knew him as Volpe."

She did not mention Darryl.

With each explanation, Jessica grew angrier as Barker would wait until its completion and then tell her, with an uncaring grin,

"My advice is to plead guilty, tell the detective everything you know, and you'll probably get off with thirty to forty-five days in a county jail and a year or two of probation."

That was *not* what Jessica had any intention of doing.

Her plan, she felt, was foolproof.

She would tell the truth and be found innocent.

Inside the Interrogation Room, the attorney and Jessica, still handcuffed, sat on one side of a six-foot table.

Brogan sat on the other.

The logbook, the schedule, a digital recorder and three plastic bottles of water were between them.

Jessica had just completed telling the detective the exact same story she had twice told her useless court appointed public defender. Telling it again had made her *more* frustrated and angrier.

"And you've been there *how long?*" Brogan asked, indicating he didn't believe her the first time he heard it.

"*Three-fucking-weeks!*" she barked. "It was just temporary until I could find *something else.*"

From somewhere inside, Jessica's anger briefly disappeared, and a deep, unexpected, heartfelt emotion came out as she held tears back from running down her face. And again, she was surprised at herself for saying "fuck" to someone in a position of authority.

"I'm near the end of a divorce. I lost my job, and I--"

"What did you used to do?"

Jessica was surprised and confused by the sudden, unexpected question. She sat up straighter, lifted her head and proudly answered, "I'm a *pi*anist."

Noticeably stunned, Brogan correctly repeated, "A *pi*anist?"

His exclamatory question made her think he either didn't believe her or that he thought lowly of her talent. Leaning forward, she angrily shot back with, "Yeah! A *pi*anist! You have a problem with that?"

The attorney put his hand on her arm to calm her down, but said nothing.

Understanding the meaning of his gesture, Jessica calmed a bit, sat back and mournfully said, more to herself than the others, "I *knew* I should've gone to Italy!"

Being that his job was to scrutinize every nuance and word of a suspect, Brogan asked, "What's that mean?"

Regretting that she said it, Jessica hung her head and replied, "Nothing. It's something I should've done instead of...never mind."

Brogan, recognizing her anguish, sat quiet for a few moments to allow Jessica time to drink some water and compose her emotions. As she did, she noticed that her attorney didn't show any concern for her well-being as he shuffled papers to-and-from his briefcase.

After acknowledging that she was ready to proceed, Brogan said, "Let's talk about Volpe."

"I told you. I don't *know* anything about him. No one there seemed to. He never came around...at least not when *I* was there. I told you...today was the first time I spoke to him. That's it." She looked down, shook her head and started rambling, "I answered the phone, I made the appointments, I put the money in the safe and wrote it..." Raising her head, she pointed to the logbook. "...in *that*." Then she glared at Brogan and told him what he already knew, "I start at one and leave at eleven. Wednesday to Saturday."

"How'd you wind up working there?" he asked with a touch of compassion in his voice that Jessica recognized.

Frustrated, she replied, "I got it through a friend-of-a-friend. Some woman named Pam used to work there. I have no idea who she is. She moved to Mexico...that's all I know." Jessica's pent-up anger surfaced as never before as she bellowed, "*I'm no prostitute!*"

The attorney again put his hand on Jessica's arm to calm her down.

Leaning forward and keeping his voice subdued, Brogan said, "Jessica, listen...between you, me..." He pointed to the attorney. "...and the eunuch here."

Barker looked at them with a raised eyebrow, but remained silent because of the eunuch he was.

The detective continued, "I've seen enough of 'em to know you're not the hooker-type. But you were slapping that guy pretty good…and you took money for it. I saw you."

Jessica leaned forward. A demented smile came across her face. It intrigued Brogan.

Raising an eyebrow and lowering her voice, she began, "You wanna hear about that? I'll tell you." Jessica leaned back into the metal chair and continued. "About five minutes before you arrested me, I was on the phone with my attorney…my *divorce* attorney. She told me my husband wants my piano." Unable to hold back her feelings, she yelled, "My *piano!*"

The attorney went to touch her arm to calm her, but before he could get close, she growled, "Back off!"

He recoiled his hand as fast as he could.

After taking another drink and several seconds to cool down, she looked Brogan in the eyes and continued. "I'm on the phone with her, and she's telling me what he wants. So I was pissed off and this guy said, 'Slap me.' He offered me money…but that wasn't what made me do it." Then Jessica laughed as she followed it with, "At *that* point I was happy to do it for *free!*"

All of the employees arrested in Diamond Jim's were questioned and spent the next fourteen hours in their cells.

The following morning, all were handcuffed and collectively brought before a judge who determined bail amounts for each of them. Five hundred dollars each was set for the bartender and locker room attendants. Each therapists' bail was set at $2,500. Jessica's was the highest at $7,500, as the judge mistakenly determined that she ran the operation.

On the walk back to their cells, Patricia sardonically told Jessica, "Unless Volpe posts bail for us soon, I'd say we're gonna have to put off my birthday celebration tonight, hon."

68

Jessica heard her…but she was too confused to react because of the Twilight Zone episode she now found herself in.

Volpe's other businesses closed their doors the day after the bust. None of those questioned knew why…only that they knew the name "Volpe," but never met the man.

By Friday morning, July 10th, "The Diamond Jim Seven," as the media had dubbed them, each realized that the unknown Volpe would not be showing up to do the right thing.

Every penny Jessica had in the bank and from what she had earned at Diamond Jim's that had not yet gone toward household and legal bills was spent on her bail and to retain a criminal lawyer.

CHAPTER 9
And Look Nice For The Cameras

Mid-afternoon that same Friday, Detective Brogan sat at his desk in the Agoura Sheriff's Station reviewing files and typing notes into his computer when Captain Harrell burst in waving a sheet of paper.

"Brogan," said the Captain without any emotion.

The detective knew Harrell was the only person in the station who never knocked first.

Brogan didn't look up. "Captain. Slummin'? What brings you to *this* side of the building?"

Putting the paper to his side, the Captain replied, "I came with good news, wise-ass."

From their attitude and conversation, everyone on the force found it hard to tell if Brogan and Harrell were friends, or simply cops who could barely tolerate one another.

The detective eventually stopped typing, closed the manila file he was referencing and turned to acknowledge his superior.

"Your bust the other day." The Captain again held up the paper. "The Chief actually read my report saying this was your tenth home run in a year…and he sent it to the Mayor. It turns out the fuckin' Mayor and *all* the Chiefs said you're making 'em look good."

The Captain looked at the detective for a reaction.

There was none, so he finished what he came to say.

"So tomorrow you're getting your Lieutenant's badge."

Brogan didn't provide Harrell the expression he had expected. Actually, Brogan showed no emotion at all.

Holding up one of the files, the detective said, "Then he's not gonna be too happy when you tell him we're going to have to throw this one back."

"Throw *what* back? The Madam?" Harrell asked with astonishment and anger. "*Why?*"

Brogan sensed the short hairs on the back of the Captain's neck were standing up.

That didn't stop the detective as he replied, "Because this kid *wasn't* running the place. She really *did* just answer the phone."

As expected, Brogan pissed Harrell off with this revelation.

The detective pulled a page from the file marked "Jessica Ross Farber," handed it to Harrell and told him, "All of the employees' stories match about *everything*. They all had the same story about her...your '*Madam*.'" He couldn't help but laugh at Jessica being called a "Madam." "She was only there three weeks. She opened up at one, answered the phone, wrote all the shit in a book and on the schedule, put the money in the safe, and then closed the place at eleven. The bartender and the hooker I was with gave the same story about the Japanese guy, and the hooker's timeline of stepping out of the room coincided with the recording I made. I even reviewed their security video and it all fits."

Based on the color of the Captain's face and his breathing pattern, Brogan should have stopped there.

But he didn't.

"None of 'em have ever *seen* this guy, 'Volpe.' I just spent three-hours checking him out. First, last, nickname, alias...I'm even waiting on the Feds. But so far...nothing. I'll check with Interpol's database next. The best I got so far was that the bank everyone was paid through was via a numbered account in the Caymans. Nothing illegal about *that*...especially since they paid everyone's taxes. But it fucks *us* up as far as determining who owned Diamond Jim's and the other two places he operated."

Harrell didn't look at the paper he was handed, nor did he want to hear what his subordinate was saying. He returned the page to the detective and began reaching for straws as he growled, "You had the place staked for weeks. Nobody went in after they closed. Volpe's fictitious. He's an alibi they were told to use if they got busted. C'mon, Tom…what's so tough about that?"

Brogan grabbed another file marked "Morgue," removed a photo, then begrudgingly used a cane to get off the chair and stand, proving how much it meant to him to get his point across to the higher ranked officer.

As he reached across the desk to present the photo, and before Harrell could look at it, Brogan explained, "The place was leased to a Pamela Sorel. The landlord said she paid the rent a year in advance…in cash."

Harrell looked at the color 8x10 photo and winced as his subordinate continued.

"She washed up on a beach in Playa Las Animas two weeks ago with her throat cut. It's hard to tell, but I think she was the receptionist when I first went there a few weeks ago."

Undeterred, Harrell returned the photo to Brogan and indignantly retorted, "The Madam's prints are on the cash. The names and appointments are in her handwriting. That's her on the phone taps. You heard what she was saying. What are you not getting?"

Holding his ground, Brogan replied in kind, " *That was her job, Captain.* Sound sexy, make appointments, take the cash. There's nothing illegal about that. And most of all, she wasn't in on what was going down inside. At worst, she's an Accomplice. But *a Madam?*" Again, he laughed at using that word to reference Jessica. "Not this kid," Brogan uttered as he slid the photo into the Morgue file. He returned to his seat, looked at the Captain and said, "So if they're gonna give me a promotion, then it should be for a job well done…not for busting Jessica Ross Farber. It's Volpe we should be going after."

None of it mattered to Captain Harrell, which showed in his acerbic question, "Am I wrong, or didn't your report say she was smackin' the shit outta some guy and you saw her get paid for it?"

Even with the tension in the room, Detective Brogan again couldn't help but laugh as he gave his response.

"Now that's a funny story, Captain. The guy she was slappin'… even *his* story matched the others. She was on the pho--"

"It doesn't matter, Tom."

By the use of his first name, Brogan knew that despite his findings, and regardless of what he had to say, higher powers were driving the Captain's actions.

"The Mayor's favorite D.A. is on it, and she's going in-for-the-kill," Harrell told the detective. "It's the kind of bust and headline they want. That's it! Deal with it."

As the Captain made his way to the door, he gruffly said, "She was in the wrong place at the wrong time. Now she's gonna take the fall…a *big* fall. That's the way it goes…and that's the way it's *gonna* go." Looking contrite, he continued, "It's not me, Tom…it's the Chiefs and the Mayor. You wanna fuck with the upper-echelon and lose your job? Be my guest. Otherwise…" He stopped at the door, turned 'official' and said, "Be in my office at noon tomorrow for your badge, and look--"

"Tomorrow's *Saturday*. It's my day off," the frustrated detective interrupted.

"Tell that to the Mayor…and look nice for the cameras."

Harrell departed as Brogan sorrowfully examined Jessica's file.

CHAPTER 10
And Please…Don't Let *Anyone* Take My Piano

The northwest San Fernando Valley morning of Wednesday, July 15th, 2015 was cloudy, causing Jessica to start the day in the same funk she had been waking up to since the bust a week earlier.

"Suz," she said into the phone as she held back tears while trying to eat a simple breakfast and drink a cup of coffee, "I need someone to talk to. Can you come by? Soon? *Please?*"

She didn't tell Suzanne she was the sixth call that morning. She had asked the same questions of other friends…but each gave poor excuses for not being able to come by. Jessica knew it was because the TV, radio and newspapers had been referring to the innocent and moral Jessica Farber as, "The S&M Madam."

She once tried to call Leon, but stopped prior to pressing his number's last digit. She had also been too embarrassed to call Charlie or Constance.

Overnight, her few remaining sticky-fingered piano students stopped coming.

Even the pianist herself hadn't touched her beloved instrument since returning to the apartment after paying her own bail.

Suzanne finally made her way to Chatsworth by 3:30PM. The clouds had passed, the sun was high in the sky and the temperature lingered in the mid-70s.

It was odd not to see the apartment's windows open, but Jessica didn't want anyone outside to overhear what was being said.

The two friends sat on the living room sofa. Suzanne was shocked at Jessica's drained appearance. There was no sparkle in her eyes. She was cried out.

"I can't believe it, Suz. *I can't believe it.* I spent *everything* on bail and my attorney. He said I might go to prison, Suz. *To prison!* No matter what he says to the court…it's as if they don't want to hear it. They don't believe me about Volpe. They don't believe it was just a job."

She had repeated the same words in her head hundreds of times since her criminal attorney told her what to expect. Each time she said it to herself, it ended the same way…she would begin crying, It would start with a slow stream and escalate into outright bawling with a torrent of tears.

Suzanne sat there devastated and crying. She took Jessica in her arms and said, "I'm so sorry I got you into this, Jess. I wish there was *something* I could do. *Anything!* I'm so sorry."

"You gotta help me," Jessica said in desperation. "You've got to find out *who* Volpe is…and *where* he is. Can you ask your friend who got me the job?"

Suzanne kept her head behind Jessica's, and with a false promise, replied, "Pammie? I'll try, Jess. But no one's heard from her since she moved to Mexico."

Jessica pulled her head back to see Suzanne's face, who still had tears dripping from her eyes, and forlornly said, "Stay here."

"Huh?" came the friend's quick response.

"My apartment. Please. You've been looking for a new place for *forever.* Stay *here.* I need you to keep all my things safe. They're all I have left. Everything in here. I don't know what to do *with* them, and I don't know what I'd do *without* them. And please…don't let *anyone* take my piano."

The two women stared at one another. Suzanne nodded.

Jessica fell quiet. She leaned into her friend's…her *best* friend's arms, and this time wept grateful tears, instead of tears of sadness and shame.

CHAPTER 11
I...Am...Innocent!

By Thursday afternoon, December 10th, 2015, the trial for the employees of Diamond Jim's who were busted on July 8th was coming to a close in L.A. County's Metropolitan Courthouse.

Judge Nancy Henline presided. The jury consisted of an equal number of men and women. On the prosecutions' side sat the female D.A., the male Prosecutor and his assistant.

Jessica, Patricia, Debbie, Tia and three other therapists and their attorneys sat at four tables on the defense side.

Brogan sat in the audience on the prosecution's side. Suzanne was also there and sat as close as possible to Jessica to offer her friend hope and support. Over the next few hours, Judge Henline heard the last of the testimonies and rebuttals before ordering the jury to deliberate.

It surprised the judge and *both* teams of attorneys that it only took two hours before everyone was called to the courtroom. The women and their mouthpieces stood as they watched a small sheet of paper go from the jury foreman to the bailiff and then to the judge...who read it without raising her head.

"Patricia Ketchum, Debra Johnson, Carly Mocco, Lisa Barlow, Dolores Robbins and Tia Nash, by the laws of this state, you've been found guilty of prostitution." She banged the gavel to make her words official. "Jessica Farber, by the laws of this state, you've--"

Jessica's attorney interrupted with, "Ross, your honor."

As if disgusted by having to look in the women's direction, the judge raised her head and gruffly asked, *"What's that, counselor?"*

The attorney stepped forward, held up a document and replied, "For the record, at the time of the arrest my client was married and her last name was Farber. But, uh…as per her divorce attorney, her divorce was finalized yesterday and she's returned to using her maiden name…Ross. Jessica Ross, your honor."

Jessica's head dropped as she heard about her life. A life she now hated.

Sadness enveloped Suzanne, knowing she was responsible for getting her friend into this mess. Even Patricia looked at Jessica and visibly expressed how bad she felt for the woman she knew was innocent.

The judge lowered her eyes and continued.

"Jessica *Ross*. You've *also* been found guilty of one count of prostitution, in addition to one count of pandering, and for operating an illegal enterprise for the use of prostitution." She took a short breath, then told the courtroom, "Sentencing will take place in one week."

With that, Judge Henline again slammed down her hammer.

Jessica went numb as three bailiffs began to escort the ladies away.

Patricia and Suzanne were openly crying for their friend.

Exactly one week later, on December 17th, the sentencing hearing took place, again with Judge Henline presiding. Once again on the prosecutions' side sat the Prosecutor, his assistant and the D.A. who had been pushing for the heaviest penalties for all those involved.

The seven defendants and their attorneys sat at the same four tables as they had a week earlier.

Brogan and Suzanne were, again, in the audience on opposite sides.

Repeating her performance, Judge Henline spoke without raising her head from the paperwork before her.

"Patricia Ketchum, Debra Johnson, Carly Mocco, Lisa Barlow, Dolores Robbins and Tia Nash, according to the penal code of this state, I hereby sentence each of you to four months incarceration in the county facility for women, effective immediately." She banged the gavel, again making her words official. "Jessica *Ross*, according to the penal code of this state, I hereby sentence you to three years in a state penitentiary for women." The judge raised her eyes from the paper, looked at Jessica with disdain and growled, "Effective immediately."

With that, she again slammed down her gavel, rose from the bench and walked toward the door to her chambers.

It was over.

The courtroom was silent.

Again, Jessica went numb as three bailiffs escorted the ladies away.

A few minutes later, Suzanne lit a cigarette as she walked down the front steps of the courthouse and made her way to a parked and running Porsche, then opened the passenger door and slid inside. A man was sitting in the driver's seat. She leaned over and kissed him as the car pulled away.

Forty minutes later the backdoor of the courthouse opened. The seven newly convicted women were handcuffed to five others as they stepped into the sixty-four-degree cloudless day.

Eight officers escorted them toward a large police transport parked thirty feet away.

Between the courthouse and the transport were a dozen reporters and news cameras.

One reporter stood to the side, looked into a camera's lens and said, "The trial of the 'S-and-M Madam' has ended. The Mayor and Chief of Police say the Madam's operation, different because it offered a 'little more for the money,' is one of many in their drive to clean up the city. They also said they're very happy with the convictions and sentences."

Reporters and camera operators pointed their microphones and lenses toward the women and tossed out questions.

"Jessica! How long did you think you could run a high-class operation like that and *not* get caught?"

Jessica kept walking and didn't respond.

"Are you protecting the identity of any well-known clients?"

Again, Jessica kept silent. The vehicle was only several feet away.

"How long have you been into S and M?"

That was it. Jessica stopped, which caused the rest of the women to cease their forward movement.

Trying to maintain a level of composure, and with the cameras and recorders going, she said, "I'm not the person you're making me out to be. This *Madam-thing* is ridiculous. *I...am...innocent.*"

A voice came back with, "Substantial evidence showed that you--"

"It's about some cop who wanted to make Lieutenant," barked the angry woman who was now the center of attention. "Look into *that!*"

A policeman stepped in front of the reporters and ushered the women into the transport as one of the cameras turned and aimed at a reporter who smiled and professionally orated, "The Mayor has kept his promise of taking a 'no nonsense' attitude toward these businesses, and he expects similar convictions from other arrests that have been made over the last few months."

CHAPTER 12
It Could've Been *Any* Of Us

In October, 1990, the Central California Women's Facility, one of the state's female-only Corrections and Rehabilitation prisons, opened for business along 640 acres of Road 22 in the town of Chowchilla, in Madera County. The quiet farm community of Chowchilla sat at 240 feet above sea level and about 250 miles north of Los Angeles.

Shaped like an elongated octagon comprised of one-story buildings, the prison was surrounded by three consecutive 35-foot tall, electrified, heavy steel cyclone fences, each topped with an endless coil of high-grade barbed wire.

The town's 11,000-plus locals lived a few miles away, with many of them working the endless acreage of farms that grow corn, soybeans, wheat, sugar beets, a variety of melons, potatoes, pears, cherries, berries, apples, grapes and peaches in massive groves that surround the prison.

CCWF, as it is referred to by its Correctional Officers, employees and those incarcerated there, had exceeded the 2,000-person capacity it was designed for, housing those convicted of all levels of crimes within its confines.

The bulk of the prisoners occupied Levels I through IV.

The Condemned Housing Section was the quarters of those who had received death sentences.

Friday, December 18th, 2015 was the day Jessica Ross was transferred from the L.A. County Women's Facility to be one of

CCWF's 2,148 occupants. Upon arrival, she was led through the Reception Center where she was given Identification Number 04071452, then processed, classified and evaluated. She was provided the mandatory orange uniform and socks, along with bras and underwear, black slip-on sneakers, blue pajamas, blue denim jeans and blue work shirts. Jessica's once beautiful shoulder length hair was cut to no more than four inches from her scalp, then she was assigned to Level IV.

Being the proverbial "fish out of water," Jessica kept to herself in the cell where she resided with five other women.

Within two days of arriving, she found the facility's library to be a refuge.

As several prisoners sat at tables scrawling handwritten letters or reading whatever interested them, Jessica found her way to a bank of five computers and began reading a tutorial. It had been quite a while since she had typed anything more than an email in her Chatsworth apartment, and she wanted to see how well she could get back into the flow, hoping that her pianist-trained fingers were still as limber as they once were.

The following day she was back at the computer typing…not as fast as she would have liked, but under the circumstances, she was grateful for the library's music CD collection which she could play through the computer and listen to via small headphones as she typed away. It was a diversion from sitting in her shared cell.

After ten minutes a timer within the computer buzzed. Jessica stopped typing and looked at the text that popped up on the screen.

"*720 words typed. 72 words per minute. 14 misspelled words. Good, but needs work.*"

Having never taken such a test, Jessica was happy with herself. She smiled, then looked around, realized where she was…and the smile disappeared.

Later that night, Monday, December 21st, after only three days behind bars and a mere four days before Christmas, Jessica was given her first taste of reality in a women's prison.

Like all of the cells in Level IV, Jessica's was large enough for the cots of its six occupants, but sparse in its function and appearance. In addition to the cots, there were three shelves which they shared to house their clothes and toiletries, but not much more than that.

It was only a half hour or so after "lights out," and Jessica couldn't sleep. She likened it to the same anxiety that kept her awake after her husband left, and after the Diamond Jim's bust.

She heard women speaking in guttural voices in the next cell, but couldn't make out anything specific until she heard a frightened woman plead, "Oh no. *No, please don't.*"

A brash, tough, evil sounding prisoner replied, loud enough for the surrounding cells to hear, "Shut up, *bitch.*" The sound of clothing being torn pierced the silence.

Jessica's nerves caused her body to curl into a fetal position. She couldn't help but hear the victim cry out, "*Oh my god! No, Karen. Leave me alone!* Leave me alo--*"

The unmistakable sound of a fist hitting someone *hard* and a body crashing onto a squeaky cot unnerved her even more.

Jessica ran to the bars and grabbed them as if wanting to help the person crying in pain and fear.

Prisoners from across the hallway watched...some in horror, others as if it were a movie being shown for their pleasure. Two of Jessica's cellmates got close to the next cell and held out mirrors to see what was happening. It sickened and scared her to know they were enjoying what was taking place.

Another cellmate, Andrea Hernandez, an intelligent, attractive 44-year-old Hispanic hardened by her time behind-bars, opened her eyes and watched Jessica in the hallway's dim light.

The evil voice growled, "I said shut the fuck up..." Another punch to the victim's face sounded as she finished with, "*Bitch!*" Then a command was given to another prisoner in the cell of violence.

"Cover her mouth."

The sound of the victim's cries deadened as someone yelled, "Go 'head! Grease it up and stick it in...stick it in *all* the way."

Jessica suddenly felt sick to her stomach.

Then came the muffled sound of a woman being painfully violated. It caused Jessica to run to the toilet in the corner and vomit. Andrea rose from her cot, went to Jessica and held her head.

"Easy, girl," came from the sympathetic Andrea. "She just wound up in the wrong cell. Fuck...it could've been *any* of us. There's nothin' we can do about it."

Jessica trembled, then continued to puke and cry. Andrea held her cellmate steady.

"I...I can't do this," said Jessica in between breaths. "I can't...I *won't* make it. Not here. I don't belong here."

Andrea leaned close to Jessica's ear, then quietly-yet-authoritatively said, "You got no choice, kid. You gotta get strong, you gotta get hard...and you gotta do it fast. Then take it with you when you get out of here."

Jessica could do nothing but weep and vomit as she heard more muffled and painful groans coming from the victim just one cell away, which were followed by more cracks of a fist against her face to quiet her.

"Atta girl," came from the rapist. "Come on...just a little more. *Take it!*"

The cot's springs continued to squeak with each thrust of whatever was being shoved inside the victim.

Breaking free of whoever was covering her mouth, the woman let out a shrill scream, which was followed by the sound of a fist hitting a jaw. It was unlike anything Jessica had ever heard before.

The victim's cries fell silent, though the springs continued to squeak...causing Jessica to cry and vomit again.

At 2:18PM on Christmas Eve, Jessica stood at a wall of payphones and placed a collect call to her apartment that was now occupied by Suzanne. The seven days of being incarcerated had already taken its toll on the innocent woman in orange prison attire. She looked and sounded terrible.

Once the call was connected, Jessica began crying. Her voice sounded *beyond* desperate.

"Suz, this place is *insane*. Please, you've *got* to help get me out of here. I can't take it."

Suzanne cried as she replied, "I'm doing everything I can, Jess, *honest*. But…" Unbeknownst to Jessica, Suzanne was sitting on the piano bench with the house phone to her ear and a cigarette hanging off the edge of the instrument next to four lines of cocaine, a razor and straw. Gashes from multiple slices of the razor were visible in the piano's once pristine wood. "…nobody knows anything about this Volpe-guy," Suzanne continued. "I called Pam in Mexico to see if she could put me in touch with him, but her phone's been disconnected."

A distraught voice replied, "You're the only one who still takes my calls, Suz. Nobody else accepts them."

"And I always will, Jess. I promise. I got your back, I swear."

"I know, Suz…I know." There were a few seconds of silence, then the prisoner softly uttered, "The guard's saying my time's up. I gotta go." Her voice lowered even more as she again began to cry and said from her heart, "Suzanne…thank you. I love you."

Suzanne hung up without replying. Her sad expression and tears disappeared as she raised the straw, snorted two lines, hit her cigarette…and smiled.

Alone in the library the following afternoon, Jessica sat at her usual computer, rapidly typing as if her piano skills had taken on a new ability. The computer's timer buzzed. Her fingers stopped and she eyed the text on the screen.

"*880 words typed. 88 words per minute. 11 misspelled words. Better.*"

She smiled…and tried to hold onto the feeling.

"You're getting good at that, Jessie."

Though Jessica didn't like being called Jessie, hearing Andrea's voice from behind surprised her and made the 'good feeling' last a little longer.

And after all, it was Christmas.

CHAPTER 13
Don't Look Back

By three o'clock on Tuesday afternoon, March 1ˢᵗ, 2016, it was 77 degrees and not a cloud in the sky over Chowchilla, nor was there a breeze blowing.

In addition to the multitude of security cameras covering every inch of the facility, armed guards patrolled the perimeter's exterior fences with assault rifles, tasers and attack dogs as they slowly cruised in vehicles that looked like well-equipped, armored golf carts.

Women gathered in groups, sitting and standing wherever they could throughout the exercise yard. Blacks. Asians. Hispanics. Middle Easterners. Native Americans. Whites…and White Trash. Many were heavily tattooed. The still air was thick with languages, bravado and cigarette smoke.

Jessica, now 33 years old, sat with a small mixed group… something not seen with the other clusters. They were *all* smoking, including Jessica. They were also articulate and spoke more intelligently than those in the other groups.

They listened as Andrea Hernandez spoke.

"Yeah well, I *never* expected to be back here." She shook her head in personal anger, then solemnly scanned the women and got serious. "But…I forgot about the curse."

Some of them chuckled, a few nodded in agreement, and others didn't believe in such things.

Intrigued, Jessica leaned forward and asked, "What curse?"

Having only been there a couple of months, Jessica was still considered a "Recent Arrival," so Andrea looked her in the eyes and filled her in.

"Nobody gives it much thought when they first hear about it. Even *I* was skeptical when I was told about the curse. But trust me...it's true. It's *real*."

Everyone got quiet...even those who didn't believe.

Andrea's face hardened as she spoke.

"Once you walk out those doors...don't look back. Just *don't... look...back*. 'Cause if you do...you're *comin'* back."

Jessica's inquisitiveness took over as she asked, "And you know this *how?*"

Andrea knew Jessica was naive to "life on the inside," so she started her story by looking beyond the barbed-wire fences and into the past.

"I had a good job waitin' for me after my first trip here. I had '*the world*' ahead of me." She cast her gaze at Jessica. "There's this bitch in here I used to fight with all the time. So...after I finished my sentence and had one foot out of the gate so they could take me to the bus station, she yelled, 'Hey, Hernandez! You *forgot* something!'" Andrea's expression changed to unresolved self-anger as she ended with, "That was it. It was too late. I turned around. I looked back."

Everyone pondered the words...even those who had heard the narrative before, whether it came from Andrea or any of the others with similar stories to tell.

Jessica inhaled on her cigarette and took mental notes as Andrea continued her story.

"About a year later, this VP of the company I was working for had me cash a four-grand check he said was for convention expenses. Next day he disappeared with nine million of the company's money. So, since I signed the check, and since I did time in here on a prior, and since they couldn't find the VP, *somebody* had to pay...so I was pegged as an Accomplice. I couldn't fight their corporate lawyers. I was fucked. It was the curse...plain and simple."

"And the bitch, the one who called your name?" Jessica asked, which caused those who knew Andrea to shake their heads.

"Still here, and there's nothin' I can do about it…not unless I wanna stay in this place longer than I need to, and her psycho-ass ain't worth it. Though, if I ever got the chance…" Andrea looked around the yard, and then at Jessica. "So, I just had to let it go."

Jessica looked deep into Andrea's eyes, nodded and said under her breath, "Don't look back."

It was around ten o'clock that night, the sign on the office door now read "Detective Lieutenant Thomas Brogan" and he was in his office. It was eight months after the Diamond Jim's bust, but he still kept a file of the case on his desk.

Perched before his computer, his eyes were transfixed to the screen as he once again accessed Interpol's database and typed in "Volpe." Then he scrolled through pages of text and a series of photos.

And once again…they produced nothing.

CHAPTER 14
La La How The Life Goes On

Outside the confines of CCWF…life continued.

In the eighteen months since he drove away from Jessica, the now 34-year-old Leon was barely holding onto his job as a graphic designer. Getting caught up in Sylvia Estrada's lifestyle, it wasn't long before his work suffered. Once free of Jessica, he and Sylvia met as often as they could. He enjoyed it even more when she'd have one of her playmates join in.

Michael Pincus, Sylvia's 75-year-old husband, had a stroke the previous year and was now homebound, and would be for the rest of his life…which thrilled his wife to no end. Thanks to the nurses that cared for Michael, Sylvia was free of any burden and was always out enjoying herself. When she *was* home, it was by choice, usually just to give her sexual orifices a rest for a night or two. At 49 years old, thanks to the gym and her sex life, Sylvia's body was in terrific shape.

Because she was married and a respected business owner who worked for the rich and famous, Sylvia was never one that required wining and dining. It wouldn't look good. Besides, she wasn't in it for the show. She was in it for the hedonistic freedom to have sex with whomever she wanted, *whenever* she wanted. Period.

Besides Leon's rent, car payments, insurance payments, credit card payments and everything else that life puts on one's finances, there were *other* expenses that were draining him…the playmates. Several months earlier Leon had started seeing some of the more erotic women that Sylvia would bring around…and many of *those* women *did* like to be taken out for lunch and dinner, and of course, their tastes leaned to the more costly restaurants.

Sylvia had no clue about these liaisons as she continued to come to Leon's apartment once or twice a week for her much required and mandatory fuck sessions.

That changed on Thursday, March 10th, 2016.

Leon had Kim Fornicola naked in the sitting position and suspended in a sex swing that hung from the bedroom ceiling attached to three heavy duty eyehooks. Kim was a 39-year-old housewife Sylvia met at the gym a few years earlier and brought her to Leon's apartment a couple of times for some three-way fun. The last time was four months ago.

Since then, Kim had come to Leon's apartment three times by herself.

With her feet wrapped in leather stirrups and her legs spread wide, her shaved opening was directly in front of his favorite part. He rubbed lube onto where he'd need it most, then slowly slid himself inside and rhythmically swung her back and forth on it.

No matter how Leon tried to cover Kim's moans and orgasmic screams, she couldn't hold back, and though Leon enjoyed hearing the audible results of his fucking, plus the wild words that would come out of her, the neighbors had already complained several times.

It was certainly due to Kim's volume that Leon didn't hear Sylvia enter the living room. She did, after all, have a key to his apartment. It only took a few seconds for the unexpected visitor to take notice of the erotic and orgasmic sounds and realize *what* was happening…but now she wanted to see *who* he was doing it *to*.

Who had been more shocked by the scenario in the bedroom was hard to say. It could have been Sylvia, who had no idea that her "private and personal fuck" was also fucking others in the swing that she had purchased for *them*. Or perhaps it was Leon and Kim, caught unawares…and by Sylvia.

Sylvia pointed to each of them and said, "Nunca más," which they knew meant "Never again." Then she walked out.

Leon and Kim would never see or hear from Sylvia again.

A week later, Leon was told to clear out his desk and given his last check and severance package.

A few days after that, Kim and all the other women he had been fucking stopped taking or returning his calls. His sex swing began to gather dust.

Within a couple of months, Leon had gone through whatever money he had, and was living on credit cards. His name was mud in the L.A. graphics industry. It didn't take long before he packed whatever possessions he had and drove back to Potter Township, Pennsylvania.

At thirty-four, Leon's hedonistic lifestyle would never be the same.

It didn't take long for Sylvia to replace the deceitful couple.

Suzanne's band, Two Ton Sun, remained popular and continued to play in clubs from L.A. down to San Diego. When she *was* at the apartment, it was usually to meet someone who wanted to purchase a piece of Jessica's furniture they had seen for sale on-line. Suzanne used the money toward paying the rent.

As time went on, the rooms became more and more bare. Though, Suzanne did keep the bedroom set as long as possible so she could bring guys there for sex.

The piano was often used to carve lines of coke on, and for Suzanne to spread herself across the top to have coke licked and snorted off her and then be serviced by her visitors.

Two months later, and because of her excessive cocaine use, Two Ton Sun replaced Suzanne with another singer.

The six women arrested with Jessica were in the third month of their four-month sentence in the Century Regional Detention

Facility, a county jail for women that was located in Lynwood, eight miles south of downtown Los Angeles.

Patricia and Debbie would often talk about Jessica. They knew she was innocent and were still stunned over how she was pegged as Diamond Jim's owner and dubbed the "S&M Madam." Yet, they also found it hard not to laugh when saying those words, knowing how ridiculous they were when referring to their blameless friend.

Charlie and Constance, Valentina's maître d' and head chef, found occasional jobs...but nothing like the Brentwood eatery they had enjoyed working at for all those years.

They would occasionally talk about Jessica. They knew she wasn't the person the media had made her out to be. Sometimes, with a little pain and sadness, they each wondered why Jessica had never called them.

CHAPTER 15
I Decide Who Does That!

Thursday, March 31ˢᵗ would be a day Jessica would retain in her mind and heart for the rest of her life…and one that would also bring home the meaning of life as an inmate.

Back in the library, several prisoners sat around reading, writing or listening to music through headphones and were happy not to be in their cells. A cigarette burned in the ashtray next to Jessica as she sat before her favorite computer, typing faster than ever before.

The timer buzzed. The text on the screen read, "*1020 words typed. 102 words per minute. 1 misspelled word. Excellent.*" Jessica smiled proudly at her reflection on the screen.

In the reflection she also saw someone coming up from behind, but couldn't make out who it was.

"What the fuck *you* grinnin' at?" the loud, tough, evil voice asked.

Jessica was stunned.

She recalled the voice.

Karen Knight was *very* muscular, tall and had tattoos covering her entire left arm up to the side of her face. She stood behind Jessica and leered down.

Jessica matched the voice and recalled the night she heard a woman in the next cell being raped and beaten. She looked at Karen's reflection…willing her fear not to show.

"You're that whore *Madam*…got caught sellin' pussy."

"Get lost," Jessica said as she continued to look at the screen and ground out her cigarette.

Karen spun Jessica's chair around, grabbed her, effortlessly stood her up and eyed her body.

Within seconds *all* the prisoners scattered.

"What do you want?" the captive nervously asked.

Karen put her large left hand on Jessica's right breast and squeezed it. Hard.

Jessica didn't move, but gave Karen a vengeful stare and growled, "Back off, bitch. *I* decide who does that!"

Karen grinned and then backhanded Jessica.

The smaller woman crashed into the computer screen. Karen reached for her, planning to do more.

"Now I'll *show ya* what the fuck I want," Karen barked as she held Jessica down by the throat. Her other hand roughly grabbed Jessica's crotch and squeezed. Hard.

As she reached for Jessica's blue denim shirt, intending to rip it off, the two women heard, "Hey *Karen!* You *forgot* somethin'!"

Before Karen could turn around, the bottom of a large wooden floor lamp smashed into the side of her head. Blood splattered as the large convict hit the floor…unconscious.

Andrea, holding the lamp, stood smiling. The stunned Jessica got onto her feet as both women scanned the deserted room.

"C'mon, Jessie, let's get the fuck outta here. It's gonna get crowded in a minute."

In her shock and confusion Jessica nervously blurted out, "I didn't do it."

"Huh? What are you talking about?"

"I'm not really a Madam," was Jessica's awkward reply.

"Like I give a fuck. C'mon…let's go."

Karen began to stir and started to raise herself up onto her tattooed arm.

Before she could lift her head, Andrea bashed it with the lamp's base again, spattering *more* blood.

Karen went down…and stayed there.

Andrea returned the lamp to its place and used her shirt to wipe off her fingerprints, then casually took the frightened Jessica's hand and led her away...but not before taking a good look at the fallen Karen.

As they exited the library and shuffled down the empty corridor, Jessica said, "I don't know how or when, Andrea...but someday, somehow I'm gonna show you how grateful I am for what you did. I'm gonna make this up to you. I promise."

"Well, right now all we need to worry about are the fuckin' security cameras. But trust me..." Andrea grinned at Jessica. "...it was my pleasure," then winked.

As if a light bulb went on over her head, Jessica 'got it,' and asked, "Was that...the *bitch?* The one who got you to look back?"

Andrea's grin grew bigger.

The two women looked at one another...and winked.

It was another long night in Tom Brogan's office.

The clock showed 11:43PM.

He was going through files stamped "Unsolved - Homicide - Female." Each one had a name. Some were recorded as "Jane Doe" followed by a number. They *all* contained photos of murdered women. Each with their throat cut.

The name "Bridget Lang" was on the next file that passed through his hands. It meant nothing to Brogan.

As he scanned one of her pictures...something triggered in him to look closer.

He stared at the image while trying to place where he may have seen her. He shrugged and moved onto the next file.

A few seconds passed before his memory kicked in. Bridget was Ingrid...the German masseuse at Diamond Jim's.

He picked up the dead German's file and read it...intently.

It took a few days of police work on the Mexican side of the border, but Brogan was patient. When he finally put the pieces together, it revealed that Bridget Lang came to America on Tuesday, May 27th, 2014, after being arrested for the third time on prostitution charges in Germany. Landing in New York City where she lived for a couple of months, she then moved to the San Fernando Valley town of Encino toward the end of that summer.

What he *didn't* find out was that not long after settling in The Valley she met a man at one of the many private 'lifestyle' parties that took place every weekend from one end of L.A. County to the other. After attending their third party together, he offered to pay for her schooling to obtain a Certified Massage Therapist certification. Should she do that, he would, "…get you a job in a classy Calabasas location where you'll make more money than you've ever made in your life."

Bridget diligently attended school and training. She put in thirty-two hours a week for sixteen straight weeks to complete her required five-hundred hours and reached that goal on Friday, January 30th, 2015.

On Monday, February 2nd she started work as a therapist at Diamond Jim's.

Early on, her friend suggested she work under a different name, seeing as "Bridget Lang" had three arrests in Germany, plus, she had already been in the country for a few months and never applied for an extended visa of any kind. With her friend's help, Bridget obtained a fake driver's license, birth certificate and passport. With those documents she acquired a real Social Security Number and card.

And voila…Ingrid Schüttel was born.

Brogan's investigation determined that five months after starting at Diamond Jim's, "the therapist" joined her friend on a trip to Puerto Vallarta, Mexico. Three weeks later her bloated corpse was found by a family sailing their 62-foot sloop about 71 miles from shore…after "Ingrid" had floated west with the current into the Pacific Ocean.

CHAPTER 16
You've Reached A Number That Has Been Disconnected

After Jessica had eaten lunch and finished her work duties in the Administration Department, she was called to see the warden. It was something that had never happened in the thirteen months of her incarceration.

She felt uneasy as she was led into Warden Carpenter's office. She had heard stories of inmates being taken there in wrist-and-ankle cuffs.

But Jessica wasn't.

The room was empty, except for the Correctional Officer who brought her there. He pointed to a chair facing the desk and Jessica sat in it. Looking in the reflection of a picture on the wall, Jessica saw a visibly harder woman. She also spotted a file bearing her name on the warden's desk.

One thing was for certain, the innocence Jessica Ross entered the CCWF with was no more.

The door to a side office opened and Warden Carpenter, a tall, black woman in her mid-50s, strode in with a smile and a plate holding a piece of cake with a single candle burning in it.

"Happy birthday, Jessica."

The prisoner was taken aback and didn't know how to react or what to say.

"Officer, you can leave. I don't think the prisoner has the potential to be violent, especially today."

The officer saluted and left the room as instructed.

Before taking her seat behind the desk, the warden placed the cake, a napkin and fork in front of Jessica while inquiring if she would like something to drink.

All Jessica could say was, "Yes, ma'am."

The warden picked up her desk phone and told whoever answered to bring a bottle of water into the office. Before either the warden or Jessica could say another word, an assistant brought one in and handed it to the bewildered prisoner.

Warden Carpenter could see by Jessica's confusion that an explanation was needed.

"Today *is* your birthday, right?"

"Yes, ma'am. January eighteenth."

"Your thirty-fourth, yes?"

"Yes, ma'am."

"Would you like to know why I brought you here today?" the warden asked as she leaned back in her leather chair.

"Yes, ma'am."

"Why don't you relax and enjoy that cake while I talk to you."

Having followed orders for the last thirteen months, Jessica quickly picked up the fork, blew out the candle, removed it and began eating as the warden opened Jessica's file. She went to the last page and began shaking her head from side-to-side.

"Since your arrival, your behavior's been extraordinarily different from those incarcerated for the same or similar offense."

Jessica stopped chewing, took a mouthful of water and respectfully responded, "Because I never did the things I'm in here for, Warden Carpenter."

Not taking her eyes from the file, the warden came back with, "You've certainly been consistent in that one belief, Jessica."

Jessica, fearful of appearing ungrateful, went back to eating the cake. Looking up from the file, the warden focused on the nervous woman sitting before her and said, "That's why, based on your performance, and the results of your aptitude and psych tests, and the fact that this is your first offense, the Review Board feels the judge was rather hard on you. Therefore, your three year sentence has been commuted to eighteen months. You're going to be released five months from today."

Jessica stopped chewing. She was speechless and near tears.

"But first," the judge continued, "You need to know there are contingencies that need to be adhered to and followed."

Somewhere inside of her, Jessica *knew* there had to be a catch… and on her birthday.

The warden stood, then turned her computer monitor around so Jessica could see the split-screen. Each was a frozen image of the prisoner sitting in front of her favorite computer. One image showed her from the front, and the other from the back. The timestamp showed Thursday, March 31, 2016 – 4:09:52PM.

Jessica took a long swallow from the water bottle.

"This security video was taken about ten months ago. That's you, isn't it?" the warden asked.

Jessica knew it was best to tell the truth and answered, "Yes, ma'am."

The video started with the tap of a key.

Jessica watched.

Within five seconds she was being approached from behind by Karen. The prisoner was overwhelmed at watching herself be so easily handled by the larger woman, then having her breast squeezed *hard*, followed by being backhanded and flying into the computer monitor, then having her crotch grabbed *hard*…from two angles.

"Here's the part I find most interesting," the warden said as they stared at the screen.

Something caused Karen to stop just before she was going to tear off Jessica's shirt. As Karen began to turn, the floor lamp's base smashed into the side of her skull, causing her to fall unconscious to the floor.

While one angle showed Andrea from behind, the other showed her face, verifying beyond a doubt that it was her.

Jessica believed the warden was going to use the video against her and her cellmate. The 34-year-old now hated her life more than she had for the past three years…ever since Leon announced that he no longer loved her, and she never knew why.

The warden turned off the video, returned the monitor to its normal position, then sat in her chair and looked at Jessica.

Jessica could not move. She could not speak. She was scared.

Warden Carpenter could see it.

Anyone could see it.

The warden authoritatively said, "This is the kind of thing I'm talking about, Jessica. This is one of the contingencies that needs to be addressed, adhered to and followed."

Now Jessica was not only scared, she was also confused.

"Karen Knight has been a thorn in this prison's side since she arrived nine years ago," the warden told her. "Yet, no one will ever testify against her even though she's raped inmates, stabbed two of them and put one in a wheelchair."

Jessica couldn't grasp where the warden was going with this.

"Since she was released from the infirmary a week after this 'accident'…" The warden emphasized the word "accident" by using finger-quotes as she said it. "…we haven't had one incident that could be attributed to her." The warden chuckled as she spoke. "It's not like she's become a model prisoner like yourself, but since that day when some inmates found her on the floor, rumors spread that there was someone bigger and crazier than Karen Knight in our facility."

Jessica took another swig of water to clear her throat so she could speak, but before making a sound the warden said, "Now, you and I know there isn't someone bigger and crazier out there, and Andrea Hernandez *also* knows it…and I want it kept that way. Why do you think we never brought the two of you in for questioning? I've *always* had this video, but I'd prefer to have the inmates believe there's a new boss in town. I can't help it if they don't know who it might be…and I'd like to keep it that way. Do you get my point, Jessica?"

Though her throat was clear, the prisoner silently-and-slowly nodded.

"You're going to be released in five months. Hernandez, assuming she doesn't do anything to affect it, has at least eight months after that before she's up for parole. I'm sure I can be helpful in my recommendation to the Parole Board...as long as the matter of Karen Knight is kept just between us. Agreed?"

"Yes ma'am," was all that came out of the respectful and appreciative Jessica.

"Now, why don't you finish that cake while we talk a bit," the older woman said, trying to relax Jessica.

The warden went to the front of the file where she would write the answers to the few questions she was about to ask...and often sympathetically.

"Jessica, do you have a place to live? Family? Friends?"

Trying not to sound depressed about it, Jessica replied, "My folks passed away years ago. I have no other family. My husband... my *ex*-husband...was the only family I had," then she took another forkful of cake. "Friends? Once I made the news, they all disappeared." She brightened a little. "I do have *one* friend. Suzanne. She's been living in my apartment, taking care of it until I get out. Though..." Jessica showed a sad side and continued, "... even *she* hasn't been there when I've called the last few times."

Warden Carpenter scanned a page in the file.

"According to this, you haven't had *any* visitors since you got here. Any reason?"

"Would *you* want to be known as a friend of the S-and-M Madam?" Jessica replied dejectedly.

The warden raised her eyebrows and gave an "I understand" nod.

"Would you like to tell your friend the good news?" the warden asked as she turned her desk phone toward Jessica. "Maybe she'll be there now."

Jessica was shocked at the warden's hospitality. She raised the handset, dialed her apartment's number and put the receiver to her ear.

It rang.

Jessica was smiling.

It rang again.

And again.

With each ring, Jessica's smile lessened.

On the fifth ring a recording answered with, "You've reached a number that has been disconnected or is no longer in service. If you feel you've reached this number in error, please dial the number again. You've reached a number that has been disconnected or is no longer in service. If you feel you've reached this number in error, please dial the number again. You've reached a number that has been discon--"

Jessica hung up the phone. She suddenly felt drained and on the verge of crying...right there in the warden's office.

"Does she have a cell phone?" the warden asked.

"Yes," Jessica responded, desperately trying to hold back tears. "But we've always talked on the house phone. I never memorized her cell number." She began to cry hard as she repeated the words in self-anger, "*I never memorized it*," and then broke down.

Warden Carpenter let her sit there as long as she needed. It was quite a while.

The apartment where Jessica had spent the happiest and saddest parts of her life was empty. Not one item of furniture remained in any of the rooms...just the holes in the walls from the nails that once displayed photos of a life that was now only a memory

Jessica's piano was gone.

CHAPTER 17
Need A Ride?

With four armed guards only 20-feet away, fourteen of Jessica's friends stood under a tent in the front courtyard of the Central California Women's Facility to say "Goodbye" to the woman being released into society.

It was already 92 degrees by noon on Sunday, June 18th… exactly eighteen months after she stepped into the prison's Reception Center to be processed. Now, Jessica was smoking a cigarette, wearing the same clothes she wore to court the day she was sentenced, and pulling a small suitcase of clothes and meager possessions as she walked with Warden Carpenter toward the steel, barbed wired gate.

Jessica dropped the cigarette onto the ground and rubbed it out with one of her shoes, saying, "That's the last one of *those*," then became reflective about her past and concerned about her future. "Everything I had before I came here doesn't exist anymore. I don't know what happened to my life…or what I'm going to find when I go looking for it."

"Sometimes you have to forget what you had. You have to forget your anger and start fresh," Warden Carpenter offered.

Jessica chuckled and retorted, "Just before I got into this mess, Warden, a man gave me some advice that's worked for me… especially in here. He said, 'Anger clouds your path to clarity and it pains your heart. You must not hold anger within. You must use it. You must release it, or…it will devour you.'"

Impressed, the warden replied, "Good advice. I hope you thanked him for that."

Jessica couldn't help but laugh as she answered, "*Thanked* him? Right after he said it I smacked the shit out of his face."

It took a few seconds before Warden Carpenter joined in on the laughter.

Gaining her composure, she addressed Jessica earnestly, "Once you locate your friends and get settled, things will fall into place. You'll be playing your piano before you know it. And when you do…" The warden raised her hand, causing a guard to walk over with Jessica's leather folio of sheet music that was taken away the day of the bust almost two years earlier. "…I'm sure you'll want this."

Jessica was astounded and near tears as she took it and held it to her chest, then mustered a smile and looked at her friends.

"*Hey, Jessica!*" Andrea yelled. Then *all* her friends shouted in unison, "*Don't…look…back!*" as they waved.

Tears ran down Jessica's face, Andrea's face…*and* the warden's.

Putting the folio in the suitcase's front pouch, Jessica nodded to the guard at the gate. He radioed someone inside and the electronic bolt clicked open.

Jessica stepped through the gate and walked directly into the back seat of the Sheriff's car ten feet away. She heard the clanging of the gate as it closed behind her and the electronic lock that re-bolted it. She told the Deputy to, "Drive. Drive fast." She wanted to get as far away as possible…and she never looked back.

The twelve-mile ride from the CCWF to the Greyhound station in Madera down Route 99 was uneventful, silent and took only 20 minutes. Jessica spent the time looking out the sideview window and thinking about her future.

It was a future that started as soon as she stepped out of the vehicle and into the heat.

She had no idea if she wanted to return to the San Fernando Valley or to the farmlands of northern New Jersey.

104

In her head, all she kept saying was that she didn't have any friends or family in either location. That simple reality brought tears of self-pity and self-anger to her eyes.

If there was *anywhere* she wanted to be, it was to be reunited with her piano...the one thing she asked Suzanne to protect and save for her.

It was the only thing she looked forward to during the first thirteen months of confinement...until her birthday when she called Suzanne to find that the apartment's phone number was no longer in service.

With what little money she had, she bought a one-way ticket to the Greyhound station in San Fernando, the town for which The Valley was named. From there, she planned to take a taxi to Chatsworth, ten miles away.

It was now a little after one o'clock and the sun was high overhead in the cloudless sky. After purchasing her ticket, Jessica went into the ladies room to wash the sweat, tears and prison life from her face. Peering into the mirror, she barely recognized the woman's reflection looking back at her.

Jessica sat in the station for over an hour with nothing to read. She didn't have an electronic device to entertain her, and she had no interest in the news channel on the bus station's TV, so she walked outside and sat on a bench under a canopy to wait for the 3:10 bus to San Fernando that was to arrive in less than an hour. In the meantime, she amused herself by observing the changes in the shadow cast by her small suitcase as it stood in the sunlight.

By 2:57PM the shadow was a little longer as Jessica scanned each direction of Madera Road in search of her transportation.

There was nothing approaching except the occasional car, truck or SUV.

By 3:22PM the shadow had moved further.

There was still no sign of a bus coming from any direction. Frustrated, Jessica walked inside to ask the ticket agent for an update, but the best response she could get was, "That bus is *never* on time. There could've been an accident and it's sittin' in a five-mile traffic jam for all I know. Besides, it's Sunday, and sometimes those drivers go right past the freeway exit and forget to stop here entirely. It'll get here…eventually."

By 3:42PM the shadow had grown even further toward the east.

Jessica was *very* frustrated, sweaty, sad…and alone. She couldn't wait under the canopy any longer. She needed to get out of the heat.

As she stood to grab the hot handle of her suitcase, a new, black Cadillac Ciel pulled up to the curb in front of her. The passenger window went down and the handsome black man inside asked from the driver's seat, "Hello, sweetheart. Need a ride?"

Startled, she bent over to tell him to "Get lost," but recognized his face.

"*Darryl?* What the hell are *you* doing here?"

"I heard you were getting out today, and I *do* owe you a favor or two, Jess. So I figured I'd start you off with a ride to wherever you're goin'. I'm sorry I just got here. I had no idea how far Chowchilla was from L.A. even *with* the GPS, and it took longer than I thought. When I got there they said you were released around noon and this was where they dropped you." Then he smiled and asked, "So… where you goin'?"

Jessica unexpectedly turned stern and replied, "Thanks, but no. I don't want anything to do with you people…or *anyone* that had to do with Diamond Jim's."

"That's good," he quickly said. "'Cause *I* don't have nothin' to do with them either. Once the shit hit the fan, I went out and started a limo business."

She wanted to believe him.

He gazed at the road in front of him, then into the rearview mirror and tried again.

"I don't see no bus comin' and the thermometer says it's a hundred-and-three. So…where you goin'?"

She hesitated, then caved.

"Italy," she laughed. "But seeing as I'm broke, I don't think I'll be leaving the country for a while…" She held up her ticket to San Fernando and said, "…I'm heading back home. Or what *used to be* home."

"Ain't you lucky! I just happen to be goin' that way."

Before she could say anything, he got out of the car.

"Let me throw that in the trunk while you go get your money back on that ticket."

While she was inside, Darryl put her small suitcase in the trunk and waited under the canopy. When she returned, her driver opened the passenger door and Jessica slid onto the new leather and air-conditioned seat. It felt good.

The Cadillac's GPS said it was 224 miles to Jessica's Lemarsh apartment and that it would take at least three-and-a-half hours to get there. However, once they traveled twenty-five miles south, Darryl decided it would be a good idea to stop and eat in Fresno.

Jessica was grateful for the idea as she hadn't eaten since breakfast in the prison.

As she devoured her first real hamburger, fries and a Coke since her sentencing, she asked, "So…how did you hear?"

Darryl gave a laugh and a sly smile as he answered, "C'mon, honey, you were news going *in*, and you're news comin' *out*. People are still talkin' 'bout you and what went down."

"What do you mean?" came her puzzled reply.

"You're like some sexy folk hero back in L.A.," he declared with a level of respect. "You're this innocent, college-educated-white-girl that got into 'the biz.' I've heard six-or-seven versions of 'why.' I know none of 'em's true. But the next thing you know, they're saying you ran this wild sex club and would whack the shit out of Oriental executives for big money."

Jessica's mouth opened wide in disbelief as Darryl continued.

"Now *I* know it's bullshit, and *you* know it's bullshit. But to those people in the lifestyle, you're some kind of fuckin' legend. *Literally!*"

It was just about six o'clock when they left the restaurant and returned to Route 99 South with another three hours to go.

Darryl's right hand reached for the audio controls as he offered, "I remember how much you liked your music. I got satellite radio with whatever you want. Anything special?"

Before he could turn it on, she sadly and uncharacteristically replied, "No thanks. I just want to relax and think. Maybe someday…maybe someday I'll enjoy my music again. Maybe. But not now."

Around 8:15PM, Jessica was looking at the scenery as it passed outside the car's windows. The sun was going behind the mountains to the west as she softly said to Darryl, "I never forgot how beautiful the sunsets were back here."

With less than an hour before they would get into The Valley, the driver asked, "Any idea where you wanna go?"

It took longer than usual for her to reply because she needed to think about what to say, and when she did it was hard for her to say the one word.

"Home." Her eyes filled with tears, though she held them from running down her cheeks. "Or at least what *used to be* home. I've got to find out where Suzanne went and what happened to my things." Then she looked at him and asked, "You don't know her, do you? Suzanne Ariza? She's a singer. Her band played at The Zone all the time. Two Ton Sun?"

Darryl looked forward and thought about it as he drove, then shook his head, "Nope. Don't sound familiar."

Jessica hid her disappointment by changing the subject.

"So…limos?"

He proudly fondled the steering wheel and replied, "I got four stretches that run pretty much all the time. I'm keepin' my nose clean and I'm doin' okay."

She smiled for the first time since leaving the CCWF and said, "Good for you, Darryl. Good for you."

CHAPTER 18
Where's Volpe?

It was 9:12PM when Darryl's Cadillac parked in front of Jessica's Chatsworth apartment. He just barely put it in "Park" before she opened the door, ran up the steps and rang the bell.

Darryl watched from the front seat as a man in his 30s answered the door holding a small child in his arms. The desperate Jessica quickly started asking questions and tried to look inside to see if her piano was there. Darryl could see the man responding by shaking his head and shrugging his shoulders. It was only a couple of minutes before he didn't want to answer any more questions and closed the door on the despondent woman.

Jessica sorrowfully made her way down the steps. As she approached the car, Darryl could see the tears streaming down her cheeks. She was overcome with heartache and couldn't speak.

Darryl stayed silent as he started the car and drove out of Chatsworth.

Cruising along the 118 Freeway, he broke the silence.

"I had a feeling things weren't gonna turn out the way you expected. They never do when one gets out of the joint." Then he pointed to the glove compartment and said, "Open it."

Unsure why, she did as instructed.

Inside was a letter envelope.

She looked at him.

"Take it, girl. It's for you," he said while keeping his eyes on the road.

Opening it, she was astonished to find it filled with $100 bills.

"Ten grand. Not enough to put you in the good life, but it'll get you some new clothes and a place to sleep."

His passenger was stunned *and* puzzled.

"How did you get this kind of money, Darryl?" she asked before accepting it.

"Like I said, these cars have been very good to me." Any hint of humor in his voice disappeared as he said with sincerity, "Look, Jess…you kept quiet. You kept my name out of it. You saved me from payin' a lot more than *that* to some thievin' lawyer. You may've even saved my ass from doin' time, too. Just take it. That envelope and this ride are the least I could do."

Closing the glove compartment, she gripped the envelope tightly and allowed the tears to flow freely, only this time they were tears of gratefulness. Somewhere from within her broken, shaken body came the words, "Thank you, Darryl. Thank you," over and over again.

The Cadillac made its way to The Beverly Garland Hotel on Vineland Avenue in North Hollywood, a legendary hotel wedged between the 101 Freeway and the Los Angeles River. Darryl drove the car up to the entrance, where they were immediately met with valets and bellhops.

Darryl popped the trunk. Jessica's one-and-only bag was placed on a cart…ready to be taken into the lobby.

As a valet opened her door, Jessica asked Darryl, "How do I get in touch with you?"

He reached into his jacket pocket, pulled out a business card and handed it to her.

That was when she turned serious and unexpectedly asked, "Where's Volpe? *He's* the one that owes me. He owes me *big* time."

Without missing a beat, Darryl answered, "He's gone, girl. After the bust, word on the street was that whoever he answered to…off'd him."

Disappointed, Jessica softly muttered, "That's a shame. I had some plans of my own."

She leaned over and kissed Darryl on the cheek.

"Thank you, Darryl. Thanks for picking me up…and for this," she said, raising the envelope in her hand.

Then she slid out the door and stepped away.

A few days later, Jessica wore new clothes. Nothing fancy because she had to make Darryl's money last. She wore them to an audition at a local restaurant.

The manager led her to an upright piano and said, "So…let's see what you got."

She cordially smiled, sat on the bench, opened her music folio and began playing. It bothered her immensely that she was rusty and had hit several bad notes. Under her breath, with each mistake she'd say, "Shit" to herself.

The manager was clearly unimpressed.

He shook his head and thanked her for coming by.

CHAPTER 19
Have You Been Convicted Of A Crime?

Bright and early the next day, Thursday, June 22nd, Jessica started her job search.

Behind a desk in the lobby of The Right Choice Temp Agency, the receptionist was reading a magazine. Two other hopefuls with pens poised over clipboards balanced on their knees were filling out applications.

Jessica, dressed in her 'court clothes,' walked in and went to the receptionist who, engrossed in the latest People Magazine, didn't raise her head.

"Excuse me."

The receptionist looked up disdainfully, not hiding the fact that her job wasn't nearly as interesting as celebrity gossip.

"I called about the--"

Before Jessica could finish her sentence, a clipboard and pen were thrust at her.

"Fill it out, then bring it back with a resume," the receptionist said tersely as she returned her eyes to the printed pages.

Taking the clipboard, Jessica mustered some courage and responded, "I don't have a resume."

Dispassionate and disinterested, the receptionist told her, "Just list what you've done," as her focus remained on the glossy photos before her.

Jessica sat and balanced the clipboard like the others and began to fill out the three-page application. In the middle of the second page she suddenly froze. Her hand shook and her fingers tightened on the pen. Her breathing became erratic as her eyes glared at the question, "In the last 5 years have you been convicted of a crime?"

She nervously put the pen to "Yes," then quickly circled "No."

Jessica approached the receptionist and held out the clipboard with her completed application, noting that the employee was now engrossed in a second magazine. Annoyance flashed on her face as she raised her head, accepted the paperwork, then scanned it and responded accordingly.

"Let's see. UCLA college grad. Good. No job in the last two years. Bad. And before that you were a...pi*a*nist?"

Jessica respectfully corrected her.

"A *pi*anist."

"Whatever." The receptionist looked at another line and suspiciously asked, "You type one-hundred-and-two words a minute? Where'd you learn to do that?"

A bit of sarcasm came out in Jessica's reply as she raised both hands and wiggled her fingers, "Music school. Coordination. It's all in the fingers."

Unimpressed, the receptionist put the application on a pile of others and said, as if by rote, "We'll call if you meet the requirements of any available positions."

Anxious for the opportunity...*any* opportunity, Jessica aggressively came back with, "I'd like to start interviewing as soon as possible. I'm not picky. I'll do any job. Any *legal* job."

The receptionist slid the company's business card in front of her.

"They'll get back to you."

Dejected, Jessica gave her a "Thanks" and walked out the door.

The receptionist went back to reading the magazine.

CHAPTER 20
Erotica!

Over the next few days Jessica registered with four more temp agencies, and though the applications slightly differed, each one had the same "In the last 5 years have you been convicted of a crime?" question. And each time, she couldn't bring herself to circle "Yes."

This lie was hard for Jessica. She had lived her life being honest to everyone...including herself. Nevertheless, her time in prison brought the realization that in the last three years, all the pain she endured was the result of others who hadn't been honest with *her*. They put her in harm's way *knowing* she would be hurt.

Leon Farber.

Suzanne Ariza.

Volpe.

She justified circling "No" by telling herself, "Answering that question honestly would mean I wouldn't get a job, and I need one to do what's right so I can get back on my feet."

Jessica was also a realist and knew it could take some time to *get* that job, so while still having the bulk of Darryl's money, she found a cheap studio apartment in North Hollywood. Then, in the last week of June, she got a job as a waitress at a diner a couple of blocks from her new address.

Waiting tables on the afternoon of Monday, July 3rd, the grouchy, frumpy woman sitting in one of Jessica's assigned booths dropped her half-eaten burger on the plate and yelled as the server passed-by, "*Hey!* I ordered this *medium!* It's *well done!* No wonder it took so long. I'm *starving*. Bring one that's *cooked right!*"

Picking up the plate, Jessica sighed, "Sorry about that. Could-a sworn you said 'well.' I'll get another one. That's with everything, right?"

Not waiting for the woman's response, Jessica walked into the kitchen and stuck an order-slip onto the wheel. Rosie, the manager, confronted her as she turned.

Rosie appeared to be about 50. She was short, round and gave the impression of a woman with a heart of gold, but in spite of her kindness, she had been known to kick the biggest men out of the diner on their asses for acting inappropriately.

"Hey Rosie, I made a mistake on an order. She wanted--"

"No you didn't, kid. She pulls that crap from time-to-time with the new help. Gets a free half-a-burger out of it. Next time, she's out on her ass." Then she grinned and continued, "You'll learn the regular creeps fast enough."

"I can handle it," Jessica assured her.

"Hope so. You're good, and I don't want you scared off," the manager replied with warmth and sincerity in her voice and smile.

A bell rang, alerting Jessica that an order was ready.

It was the Fourth of July.

Outside the rundown apartment complex where Jessica now lived, and as young kids walked by, a man in his early 30s exchanged a baggie of powder for cash with a stoner. The cars parked along the curb were dirty and old. Incongruous with the neighborhood, piano music wafted through an open window...albeit, with the occasional mistake.

Inside the first floor apartment, Jessica, off from work that day, sat on a mattress that laid on the floor in the middle of the bare room that only contained a lamp, a weathered coffee-table and a clock-radio. Playing a cheap, used electronic keyboard, she was *very* frustrated with her performance. She played the piece again, made the same mistakes, smashed her fists on the keyboard…then yelled, "*Fuck!*"

She was doing whatever she could not to think about the second anniversary of the bust at Diamond Jim's that was only four days away.

Late the following morning, Jessica was getting ready for her afternoon shift at the diner. Having a few minutes to spare, she sat on the mattress practicing scales and finger exercises on the keyboard, though was *still* frustrated by her performance.

Seeing a temp agency business card laying on top of the keyboard, she picked up her cell phone, which was the cheapest model one could buy. She dialed the number and began to speak once someone answered.

"Good morning. This is Jessica Ross. I was in several days ago. I just wanted to know if you've had any luck getting me an interview." She listened as the person spoke, then, "Oh. Uh-huh." Jessica became overcome with gloom and despondency, then shamefully replied, "No, I didn't know I circled the wrong--"

The person spoke again. Jessica's eyes filled with tears.

"But I *wasn't--*" She listened again, then hung up and cried.

After washing her face for the second time that day, Jessica went to work and attempted to put more-than-was-humanly-possible out of her mind. Try as she may to smile for her customers, her thoughts kept reflecting on her situation and the conversation with the temp agency. It was *very* hard for her to stay upbeat.

By 4:30PM, with plates of burgers and fries on her arms, Jessica maneuvered to a table with three heavily tattooed punks in their mid-20s. One male and two females.

The male belligerently bellowed, "I need another Coke."

With an equally disrespectful attitude, one of the women barked, "Me too," then gave Jessica the once over…but said nothing.

As Jessica walked away, the three leaned toward each other whispering.

Rosie walked up to Jessica as she filled the two glasses at the soda dispenser and offered, "Lucky you. Want me to put someone else on 'em?"

"Nah, they're okay. I got it."

Rosie gratefully smiled as Jessica returned to the table and placed the sodas in front of the punks. Once again, the woman stared at the waitress and asked, "Do I know you? You look familiar."

Jessica eyed her in detail, shook her head...then reconsidered and inquired, "Ever go to a place called The Zone?"

"Yeah, a couple of times. But it closed about a year ago. Where you been?"

"Away," the waitress fired back, then got hopeful. "Do you know a girl named Suzanne Ariza? She sings with Two Ton Sun. They played there all the time."

Jessica looked at them, eager for a positive answer. All they did was shake their heads and eat the food before them. The waitress, sullen, walked away.

Seeing an empty table that needed cleaning, she stopped to wipe it down. A newspaper laying on the chair caught her attention, so she picked it up for a closer look.

There was a half-page ad for an art show that coming Sunday, July 9th, called "*EROTICA!*" at The Lomax Art Gallery in Beverly Hills. It showed a picture of Patricia with the last name of Callahan as the featured artist. Jessica was dumbfounded. She carefully tore the ad out, folded it and put it in her pocket, then began wiping down the table.

Suddenly, the female punk's recall kicked in.

She yelled, "*I got it!*"

Jessica turned and looked at the punk who was now pointing at her.

"You were that chick on the news!" The restaurant patrons looked at Jessica. "You're the *Madam!* The *S-and-M Madam!*"

Jessica froze. Fear numbed her. She could hear people mumbling and see them staring, whispering and nodding.

The punk continued the barrage with, "You're the one that ran that massage place!"

The other woman in the threesome threw in, "What are ya doin' *here?*"

The male yelled so everyone could hear, "If I don't leave a tip, you gonna smack me?" That was followed by one of the women answering, "No! You gotta *pay her* for that!"

That was it.

Jessica's mettle went up. She had endured enough over the past three years and wasn't going to take anymore. She threw back her shoulders, rushed toward their table, reached out and grabbed both the loud woman and man by their shirts. Pulling them to her, she got in their faces and growled, "You want me to *smack you*, assholes?" Fear enveloped them. She looked at the man and laughed, "You don't look like you could afford me *anyway!*"

Jessica released her grip, pushed them back into their seats, grabbed their Cokes, poured them on their heads, then turned and headed toward the front door. Passing Rosie on the way, the manager asked, "You okay?"

A *very* angry Jessica quietly replied, "No," then departed.

Patrons watched from the window as she walked down the street, her head held high in spite of the awful churning in her stomach.

It only took a few minutes to get to her apartment. After slamming the door behind her, the distraught Jessica fell onto the mattress, looked at her possessions and considered her life…then curled up and cried.

It also caused her to realize what the pent-up anger from her time in prison could bring out.

Later that evening in a coffee shop on Ventura Blvd, Jessica was sitting across from Darryl.

She looked like shit.

"It's gonna happen, sweetheart. People are gonna recognize you," Darryl sympathetically offered.

"I…I never thought this could happen to my life, Darryl. I went to *prison*, for Christsake!"

"Do you…do you need more money?" he asked.

He could hear how grateful she was in her reply.

"No. I still have some. I can't take more. I'm making the rent from the diner. Rosie's great and she doesn't seem to care about… you know." She took a deep breath, a sigh and a sip of coffee, then said, "I just want to find Suzanne and all of my things. Especially my piano."

Reaching into her purse, Jessica pulled out the ad and handed it to him. He unfolded and scanned it.

"Look familiar?" she asked.

He didn't recognize Patricia. And then…he did.

They scrutinized the half-page ad.

"This Sunday is her birthday," Jessica told Darryl. "Two years ago on that date we were going to have dinner at Don Cuco. Well… *that* never happened."

CHAPTER 21
My Name Is…Mario. Mario Vissani

From inside The Lomax Art Gallery on North Robertson Blvd, The Dave Brubeck Quartet's "*Take Five*" flowed out the front door and past the posters that read "Patricia Callahan's *EROTICA!*"

Inside the main gallery, a few dozen people mixed and mingled. Women in provocative-yet-elegant lingerie served hors d'oeuvres. Fashionably erotic artwork hung on the walls and sat on easels. Patricia, stylishly dressed, circulated among the crowd.

Visible through the large front windows, Jessica stepped from a cab and perused a poster at the door before entering. With her hair styled and a new dress, Jessica looked better than she had in a long time…except for a piece of lint that clung just above her left breast.

Nervously, and in spite of being riddled with anxiety, she went right to the bar.

"A Rémy Martin, please."

The bustier-clad female bartender nodded and prepared the drink.

Jessica turned and scanned the room, the people and the paintings, making note of how the well-known jazz standard in the background enhanced the atmosphere.

From behind her the bartender said, "Madam, your drink."

Absorbed in the environment, Jessica didn't hear her, so the bartender repeated herself, this time a little louder, "Madam?"

Jessica quickly spun around and angrily looked at her.

"What's *that* supposed to mean?"

Cordial and apologetic, the bartender responded, "Your drink…miss."

Jessica calmed down and felt foolish. "Oh...sorry."

The bartender slid the snifter toward Jessica as she opened her purse to get money for a tip.

A handsome man with a suave Italian accent stepped from behind Jessica and said, "You obviously know the appropriate drink for an event such as this."

Jessica turned to see Mario, a very well-dressed, early 40s, dark-haired, dark-skinned Italian...only an inch or two taller than she.

His hand reached and put five dollars into the tip jar as he said, "Please, allow me, cara mia," then he looked at the bartender and said, "I will have one, also."

The bartender again nodded and prepared the drink.

Mario looked at Jessica. As he spoke, she watched with concern as he, without asking, gently removed the lint from her dress and discarded it. She was momentarily captivated...even more so as he explained why cognac was the right drink for such an event.

"As you walk from one painting to another you must cup the snifter..." Mario put the snifter in her hand. He then controlled her hand as he swirled and raised it to her nose. She inhaled. "...letting the warmth of your body heat its contents, exciting it, releasing its essence...its aroma..." Controlling her arm, he slowly, sensuously, lowered the snifter to her mouth, making its rim touch her skin and lips along the way. Then he removed his hand from hers. "...and taste."

She sipped the cognac, smiled, then looked directly into his brown eyes.

"Buona sera. My name is...Mario. Mario Vissani."

He extended his hand. Without taking her eyes from him, she put the snifter on the bar and slowly shook it. It was hard for her to speak.

"Jessica."

"You are an admirer of this work?" he asked.

"I...I came to see the artist." Jessica gave a slight laugh and continued, "We knew each other...briefly...a couple of years ago."

"Ah," he replied, then scanned the room. "An interesting crowd, si?"

She *also* scanned the room as the bartender slid Mario his snifter of cognac.

"It's certainly different from the one *I'm* used to seeing every day," she answered with a twinge of sarcasm.

Mario took his snifter, inhaled the cognac's aroma, then raised it for a toast.

She was intrigued by his style and class.

"A noi," he proclaimed.

"Which means?"

"To us."

She smiled.

They tapped their snifters and drank.

Just then, Jessica saw Patricia in the crowd.

Respectfully, she said, "Please forgive me, Mario. I see my friend and we have some old times to catch up on." She gave him a school-girl smile and shyly imparted, "Maybe we'll bump into one another again...maybe."

Mario took her hand and raised it to his lips.

"Nothing would please me more."

Then he kissed the smitten woman's hand.

Noticeably enamored, Jessica stepped away and blended into the crowd.

Patricia stood, seemingly bored among a group of five people as she studied the room while someone attempted to engage her in conversation.

"I was at the two Getty museums recently," said the nondescript male art patron. "Except for the sunsets and modern architecture, I'm not impressed with the Center's collection. The Villa, on the other hand, is simply brilliant."

While viewing the crowd, Patricia made brief eye-contact with Jessica, who was the *last* person she expected to see, and kept scanning.

Then she stopped, returned to focus on her friend and stared at the familiar face.

The patron continued, "For a private collection, it *is* a magnificent showplace. Wouldn't you agree, Miss Callahan?"

Patricia was oblivious to the question as she and Jessica walked toward each other.

Everyone watched the two beautiful women meet in the middle of the gallery and hug.

Mario observed them from the bar.

Discreetly watching from the other side of the room was Detective Lieutenant Tom Brogan, whose hair was now longer and grayer.

The women abruptly went into Patricia's studio behind the gallery and locked the door so they wouldn't be interrupted by anyone.

The large room was full of erotic artwork in various stages of completion.

Patricia and Jessica sat at a small table with a bottle of Rémy Martin and two snifters. Their faces showed how happy they were to be together.

As they were about to toast, Jessica said, "Happy birthday, Patricia. We never *did* get to have that birthday drink and dinner together."

Stunned, Patricia exclaimed, "*You remember?* That's wonderful of you, Jess! Thank you."

"How could I forget? We were arrested the day *before*," Jessica sullenly uttered.

"None of us bought that bullshit they said about you...owning the place and being some kind of Madam," Patricia expressed with conviction. "And to give you three years for *that?* That was even *more* bullshit." Realizing three years hadn't passed, the artist queried. "We had to do our full four months. How did *you* get out early?"

124

"Good behavior, a sympathetic warden and a Review Board that felt I got screwed over. Oh…and a friend on the inside with a floor lamp."

Patricia agreed with it all, though she had no idea what the last statement meant and thought it wise not to pursue it. Deciding it was best to change the subject, Patricia eyed her friend and said, "You look fantastic!"

"It's *you* that looks fantastic!" Jessica returned, then proudly viewed the studio. "You're an artist, Patricia! You *did it!*"

Patricia humbly responded, "Once I got out of…well, you know…I finished school and got to work. I made enough to start this place, and then--"

"This gallery's *yours?*" Jessica interrupted. Patricia grinned and nodded, then Jessica inquired, "You didn't go back to…?"

"Rubdowns and hand-jobs? No. Hard work this time, Jessica… and it's legit." Patricia gave a sly smile. "I'm still selling sex. Only this time it's on the canvas." She pointed to the paintings surrounding them as Jessica's eyes followed. "And fortunately, people like them." The artist drank, laughed and confided, "You'd be amazed at how many portraits I've been commissioned to do…all in the same erotic and extravagant fashion."

Jessica cocked her glass to Patricia and they again toasted.

Before the snifters were empty, Patricia refilled them.

"If you own the gallery, who's Lomax?" Jessica inquired.

"It's my real last name."

"What about Ketchum? The one you used in court."

"Fake. Used it for years."

"You're kidding!" Jessica blurted, somewhat in shock.

"As the saying goes, Jess, '*I got a guy.*' You never know when you'll need to be someone else at a moment's notice, my friend. And you'd be amazed how easy that can happen for a few grand."

"And Callahan?"

"My professional name. Any more questions, your honor?"

"No," Jessica answered. "The defense rests...and is *very* impressed."

They shared a good laugh and drank their cognacs.

Interested in knowing how her friend was coping, Patricia earnestly asked, "So...how's life?"

"Not so easy. That whole *Madam-thing* screwed me *royally*. I lost everything, and...and I'm working at this--" Jessica reconsidered and ended it with, "Never mind."

"You know, I've heard some people speaking pretty highly about you...or at least who they *think* you were," Patricia quietly said.

"So I've heard."

"From who?"

"Darryl Bowling," Jessica replied.

"Darryl Bowling? *Security Darryl?*"

Jessica nodded.

"Watch out for him, Jess."

"Why?" Jessica asked with concern, then continued before Patricia could reply. "He's the *only one* who's been there for me since I got out. He picked me up. Gave me some money--"

"And he worked for Volpe." Patricia interjected.

"We *all* worked for Volpe." Jessica quickly retorted. "Besides, I heard he may have been killed."

"Yeah, I heard that, too. But no one knows for sure. No one knew who the hell Volpe *was*. All I know is that you were innocent and took the hit for the whole thing. The cops, the D.A., the judge...it was like they lived to nail you."

Sipping their cognacs, Patricia wrote a phone number on the back of her business card and slid it across the table.

"That's my cell. Call it...anytime," Patricia got very emotional, "And I mean *anytime*, Jess."

Jessica gave a grateful, "Thank you, Patricia," then to lighten the mood she added, "It *is* Patricia...*isn't it?*"

With a sly grin, the artist answered, "As far as *you* know, it is."

They stood, touched glasses and downed the rest of the cognac.

The crowd in the main gallery was glad to see Patricia return. She again began working the room as The Ramsey Lewis Trio's "*The In Crowd*" came through the speakers.

Jessica enjoyed hearing another familiar piano tune.

Brogan, the limp on his left side still apparent, strolled from painting to painting as he watched Jessica make her way to the front door, but not before Mario caught her eye.

She smiled as he approached.

He noticed a strand of her hair was slightly askew as he said in his deep, suave Italian voice, "I was hoping you would allow me to drive you home. If you are hungry, maybe we can stop for something."

"What makes you think I need a ride?" she asked, suspiciously.

He gently and gracefully straightened her out-of-place hair and replied, "Through the window. I happened to see you arrive by taxi. I assure you, my car is quite a bit more comfortable, and will cost nothing."

She thought for a second. The cognac was in control. Mario looked into her eyes. She melted.

"Will you speak Italian for me?" she asked.

"Se e' quello che desideri."

Jessica looked at him inquisitively...unsure of what it meant. So he told her.

"If that is what you wish."

"Can I trust you?" she asked.

"With your life, cara mia. With your life."

CHAPTER 22
My Little Puttana

Mario's black 2016 Mercedes-Benz SLK convertible smoothly maneuvered through the streets of Beverly Hills, cruising west on Sunset Blvd for a short ride before making a right onto Bel Air's Beverly Glen Blvd. Jessica had no idea where they were going, but at the moment it didn't matter. She was enjoying the summer wind in her hair and the soft jazz music coming from the radio.

Before reaching Mulholland Drive, the Mercedes turned left into the Glen Centre's parking lot that was filled with the standard array of high-end vehicles.

From the minute Mario and Jessica left Patricia's art gallery, Brogan had never been more than thirty to forty yards behind them in an unmarked car.

A short time later, Mario and Jessica were sitting at one of Fabrocini's Italian Restaurant's patio tables in pleasant conversation, eating appetizers and enjoying a bottle of Chardonnay as Frank Sinatra, Dean Martin, Tony Bennett and Jerry Vale sang in the background.

Brogan sat in his parked car watching…as an oldies station kept him company.

It was around eleven o'clock. The couple stepped from the convertible outside the apartment complex where Jessica resided, then strolled to her door.

Embarrassed, she said, "It's not a very good neighborhood."

Mario was quick to reply, "After what you told me you have been through, you should be proud of yourself for coming this far," then he stroked her cheek, leaned and kissed it.

Her eyes rolled back at the touch of his lips.

"I wouldn't do that, Mario," she moaned with a passion in her voice she hadn't tapped into in a long time. "Not to a woman who hasn't been with a man for a couple of years. It could be dangerous."

In his thick Italian accent he replied, "I will take my chances, bella." They smiled at each other, then he stepped back and asked in the most gentlemanly manner, "May I call you tomorrow?"

Jessica only had to think for a second before she nodded, then took a pen from her purse, wrote her cell number, handed it to him and said, "After six-thirty, okay? I work until six."

"Ci vediamo domani. Until tomorrow."

Grateful for the company, the dinner and the ride home, she smiled again and said, "Good night, Mario…and thank you. It was a wonderful evening thanks to you."

Jessica unlocked the door and entered the apartment as Mario said, "Ciao, bella," then walked to his car, started the engine and drove away.

A few seconds later, Brogan's car started and cruised by.

Once inside, Jessica turned on her clock radio to a station that played soft piano music. After a quick shower, she turned off the lamp and crawled onto the mattress wearing only a T-shirt and panties. As the music continued to play, she slid under the sheet and stared at the ceiling…thinking. Slowly, her hand went beneath the sheet and began to make a circular motion. It was only a moment before Jessica erotically and sensuously moaned to a touch she hadn't enjoyed since before Leon left. It was a pleasure she had denied herself for the eighteen months she was in prison.

In the affluent neighborhood of Hancock Park just south of Hollywood, construction equipment dotted the large property of an attractive two-floor home with scaffolding attached to its side.

Mario's car pulled into the driveway.

A moment later he crossed the threshold of the finely furnished living room and saw a mess. Cigarette butts filled an ashtray. A few empty beer bottles sat next to open 'take-out' containers on the coffee-table. On the end-table was a mirror with several lines of cocaine, a razor and straw.

Mario gave a sickened look as he smelled the air and scanned the disarray.

Suzanne, dressed in jeans and a T-shirt, nonchalantly entered from the kitchen smoking a cigarette.

She flirtatiously looked at him and cooed, "What took so long, baby?" as she glided over to hug him.

He reacted with disgust to the way she smelled and tried not to let her wrinkle his clothes.

Mario replied, in flawless English…no longer with an Italian accent.

"I was having dinner with your old friend."

"And? Is she still naïve? Think that bitch is stupid enough to let us use her *again?*"

Mario laughed, "Be nice. That's no way to talk about our new business partner." Then he slyly finished with, "Of course, she doesn't know that…and she *never* will."

"Little Miss Madam's reputation's gonna make us a bundle," came greedily from Suzanne's mouth. "And she won't have a clue."

"You know, my little puttana," Mario said with a noticeable level of sarcasm, "It's such a good scam…I can't believe *you* came up with it."

Suzanne was insulted, but he didn't give her time to voice her protest as he continued, "Now, clean up this place. How many times do I have to tell you? I want my home immaculate. Why do you have a problem with that?"

Angry, wired on coke and overreacting, she barked, "*Fuck you!* I hate when you get psychotic with your '*clean*' shit!" She bravely turned her back on him, strutted to the end-table and snorted a line.

Mario raised an eyebrow…not happy with what she said.

The following night, Jessica and Mario had dinner at Geoffrey's, her favorite Malibu oceanside restaurant, and a location she presently couldn't afford on her own. Drinking cognac from snifters, they watched the sun sink below the horizon.

Afterward, he drove her to Hancock Park.

As the Mercedes slowly cruised by, only the exterior lights to his home were on. The construction equipment and scaffolding were still present.

With his Italian accent, he pointed to the house and said, "Questo è la mia casa. This is my home. But as you see, I am having much work done. They began only yesterday. There will be a new roof, painting the inside, stone walkways, landscaping, and over the next several weeks everything inside will be…come-si-dice? How do you say…gutted, si? Otherwise, I would take you in." He stared at the home and continued, "I go there only for papers, business documentazione, from my office. The hotel where I stay…it is comfortable."

With that, the car rolled past the property.

A few days later, Jessica and Mario sat along the railing of a Sunset Plaza restaurant enjoying lunch and champagne. They looked into each other's eyes. It was apparent to all that Jessica was happy…as happy as she had been when she sat behind the piano at Valentina's.

And *always* like a gentleman, Mario drove her home, walked her to the door, gave her a kiss, then departed as she stepped inside.

On the days Jessica didn't work, she would go to more temp and employment agencies…entering each with a smile. Though when she left every one of them, her smile had disappeared and she looked more and more depressed and despondent.

Then there were the rare days when Jessica, with her music folio in hand, would audition for restaurants, hotels, anyplace that was looking for a pianist.

In many locations the managers would cordially smile, realize or recognize who she was, then shake their heads before she could get to the piano. In others where she *did* get to play for them, they would suggest she come back after a little more practice.

Around 7:30PM on Tuesday, July 25th, Mario's Mercedes pulled to the front of the historic Georgian Hotel at 1415 Ocean Avenue in Santa Monica. The valets opened both doors for Mario and Jessica to step out, then the car was whisked away. Jessica was wearing a comfortable blouse and skirt. Mario was, as usual, handsomely dressed in a sport jacket, a collared shirt and dress pants…and his accent was in full force.

"Because you enjoy seeing the ocean, I thought you would like to have dinner here…and to see it like you may have never seen it before," he told her as they walked into the lobby.

Mario approached the Veranda Restaurant's maître d', reserved a table for eight o'clock, then took Jessica's hand and led her toward the elevators. Jessica appeared puzzled as they waited for the next one, but his conversation diverted her attention.

"Jessica, I have a party to attend at a friend's home in a week-and-a-half, on August fifth. I am hoping you will accompany me." Her reaction surprised him. Instead of a quick "Yes," she looked worried, so he asked, "Stai bene? Something is wrong. What is it?"

Shyly and with a deep look of embarrassment, she answered, "I…I haven't been to a party in a while. Other than the dress I wore when we met, I may not have the clothes to wear to a--"

Mario cut her off, "No, cara mia. Please, leave that to me."

He stood face-to-face with her and positioned her head to accept his lips. He stopped an inch away, then their lips touched… just as the elevator bell chimed.

Their lips separated as the doors opened. He led Jessica inside, pressed the button for the top floor and placed her against the back wall. As the doors closed, he approached her. She moved toward him and they passionately embraced and kissed.

When the doors opened at the top floor, there was a man and woman wanting to enter. Mario and Jessica were flustered, smiling and disheveled as they stepped out.

Giggling like teenagers as they walked down the hallway, Mario told her, "Come. Let me show you something magnificent."

He led her to a door marked "Exit." He opened it and gently pulled her along. She looked at him…intrigued. She certainly wasn't afraid. They walked up one flight of stairs to another door. Opening it, the couple emerged onto the roof. Jessica saw the breathtaking view of the Pacific Ocean and the descending sun.

"Is it not beautiful?" he asked.

She could only nod.

From behind, Mario put his arms around her and nibbled on her neck. She closed her eyes and melted against him. His hand caressed one of her breasts. She moaned, then her eyes opened with concern.

He sensed it.

He moved his hand and took his lips from her neck.

"I did not mean to--"

"No, Mario. It's not you or what you're doing. It's…it's…"

He turned her around so they could face each other.

"No, Jessica. I understand. We will wait until you are sure, until…you are ready."

She gazed into his eyes, thinking to herself, "Is this guy real?"

"Mario, how do you know of this place…up here on the roof?"

He let out a chuckle and replied, "This is the hotel where I have been staying until my home is complete. My suite is right below us and this is the view I have every day and every night." Not wanting her to be uncomfortable, he said, "Come, let us have a nice meal."

He took her hand to lead her to the door from which they entered.

Jessica stood still and jerked him back.

Confused, he looked at her expectantly.

She seductively put her back against the door and whispered, "I'm ready."

Surprised, he asked, "Now? Here?"

Jessica answered, "Here. Now," then pulled him toward her, ravaged his face with her lips, ran her hands through his hair and drove her body into his.

CHAPTER 23
What Do You Want, Brogan?

Jessica walked into her apartment looking at the daily handful of junk mail, exhausted because she had just worked a double shift at the diner, making her oblivious to her surroundings. Without looking, she dropped her keys where the cheap coffee-table would normally be. Instead, the keys hit the floor, causing her to raise her head.

Her eyes went wide.

The entire one room apartment had been painted and carpeted, and her cheap furniture had been upgraded. A queen-size bed replaced the mattress. There was a bouquet of white roses in a vase on the new coffee-table. She began to cry.

Jessica took the card from the roses to see it read, "You like, si?"

She grabbed her cell phone, tapped Mario's number and waited impatiently for an answer.

As soon as she heard his voice, she said between sobs of happiness, "Si, I like. *Very* much."

After her Saturday, July 29th shift at the diner, Jessica paid a surprise visit to Patricia at The Lomax Art Gallery around four o'clock. The gallery's owner and an assistant were hanging a new painting as Jessica, wearing jeans and a blouse, entered. The two women happily hugged and kissed as soon as they saw one another.

Patricia pointed to the picture.

"You like?"

As she had said a couple of days earlier, Jessica responded with the same, "Si, I like. *Very* much," then added, "It's wonderful, Patricia."

"Thanks, Jessie," blushed the artist appreciatively. "And *damn!* *You* sure look happy. Wait! You got a job playing piano!"

"No...no," uttered the musician reluctantly. Then a grin came upon her face. "But I found someone who knows how to play *my* keyboard."

Patricia was happy to hear the news and again hugged Jessica.

"No shit. C'mon...tell me about him," Patricia queried, then gave a wink and asked, "It is a *him*, isn't it?"

They laughed and walked to the reception area that housed the De'Longhi espresso and coffee maker. As Patricia poured a cup of coffee for her visitor and made an espresso for herself, Jessica started her story.

"His name is Mario Vissani. Italian. *Very* nice. A gentleman, actually, and I love the way he speaks." Then came the satisfied smile. "And sexy. Sexy in a way I've never experienced before."

"Good for you, Jessica," Patricia said, happy her friend found someone to treat her well and occupy her time.

Jessica spoke wistfully, "He makes me laugh, he's respectful, and...there's something about him. Something about the whole relationship. You know how we're supposed to be attracted to the mysterious types? Well, that's Mario. Yet, he makes me feel... wonderful." She suddenly remembered something, then grinned at her friend. "You know, I met him here. At your show."

"Vissani. Mario...Vissani." Patricia thought for a few seconds as she mentally went through the guest list, then shook her head. "Doesn't sound familiar. Did he come with someone?" Jessica shook her head as Patricia asked, "What does he do?"

"Real Estate."

"You sure he's not just trying to sell you a house?"

Laughing, Jessica replied, "No. He buys properties, fixes them up and sells them. Before he came here he was doing it in Italy. Seems pretty successful at it."

"Any idea why he was at my show?"

Jessica pointed to a wall of Patricia's paintings and answered, "Maybe he likes art? Maybe he likes *your* art?"

"What's in his house?"

"Don't know. Haven't been inside yet. He's having renovations done, so he's staying at The Georgian in Santa Monica."

Patricia, curious, but not wanting to upset Jessica, asked cautiously, "Does he know about, you know, the Madam thing?"

"I told him, but it doesn't seem to be an issue…at least not at the moment."

"That's a plus, but just be careful, Jess," the artist advised.

"Working in that massage hole jaded you, Patricia."

"True. But just remember…be smart, and enjoy the good times, 'cause you never know how long they're going to last."

Jessica smiled appreciatively, then asked, "How about you? Anyone?"

"Remember? I'm on a mission. I was only in that 'massage-hole' to pay for school and bank what I could for *this* place. Fortunately, my art gets taken seriously. But then, the subject matter wasn't a bad choice, either. Sex *always* sells…in one fashion or another." Patricia placed her hand on Jessica's and continued, "Right now a relationship would just get in the way."

They looked at one another, smiled, leaned close…and kissed.

When the taxi pulled in front of Jessica's apartment at 7:50PM and she stepped from the rear passenger door, there was still another seven minutes of sunlight left. She walked in the direction of her door, but decided to turn and watch the dusk effect in the sky and its play of color and light. In doing that, out of the corner of her eye she caught the glimpse of a nondescript car pulling into a spot across the street. Subconsciously, it unnerved her when she noticed that the driver didn't get out.

She nonchalantly turned, entered her apartment…and locked the door.

The first thing she did was to turn on the new sound system that came with Mario's apartment make-over. The room filled with soothing piano music. Then she sat at the new small dining table with a pen and pad to write any information that would come from the cell phone messages she was now listening to.

"Jessica, this is Louise from Valley Employment. I'm afraid we have to cancel your interview tomorrow. It appears our background check differs from your response on the application. So--"

Jessica slammed down the phone. Frustrated, she went to the window, opened the blinds and looked at the last rays of the sun and noticed the car at the curb. The driver was still behind the wheel. She bravely stepped out of the apartment and went directly to the open window on the car's passenger side and brazenly leaned in.

It only took her a second to recognize the face, then she angrily growled, "What do you want, Brogan?"

The detective affably replied, "It's nice to be remembered. Hello, Jessica. How have you been?"

"Terrible. How did you find me?"

"I'm a detective. It's what we do." Somber and sincere, he said, "Jessica...I never thought you were who they said you were."

Jessica sarcastically tossed back, "I figured that when I saw your picture in the paper. You know, like when they made you a Lieutenant for arresting me, and when you were on the stand talking about me slapping that guy." Her voice exuded anger. "I told you what that was about. You even said you believed me. So cut the bullshit. I served my time...you got your promotion. Now leave me the fuck alone."

She stood to leave. He quickly exited the car. They looked across the hood at one another. Neither said a word until Brogan broke the silence.

"I want Volpe."

"Me too," Jessica fired back. "But I heard he's dead."

"From who?"

Jessica grinned, "Nobody." Confronting him and near tears, she asked. "If you didn't think I was guilty…why did you let me go to prison?"

"It was outta my control. The higher-ups wanted a headline… you and me were that week's winners. Besides, we couldn't find a shred of proof to corroborate your 'Volpe' story." Brogan took a business card from his jacket pocket and reached across the hood, offering it to her. "The Captain, the D.A., everybody thought Volpe was nothing but a bad alibi. If he was real, he was one smart, invisible, son-of-a-bitch."

She let what he said sink in…but it still pissed her off.

His hand was still extended with the card.

"Can you tell me anything about him? His people?" Brogan pressed.

"I told you everything I knew two years ago. I did my time, Brogan. I don't have to answer your questions anymore. So get lost and go play cop."

"Please, Jessica, take this," he brought the card closer to her. "If you change your mind…or if you need anything."

Jessica thought for a second, took the card, turned, then headed back to her apartment.

Brogan watched…but the feeling of his personal guilt for putting her in prison stayed with him.

As Jessica entered the apartment, her phone was ringing.

Still pissed off, she tossed Brogan's card onto the bed and angrily answered the phone, "Hello?"

"Ah, cara mia."

Hearing Mario's voice and romantic accent, she tried to calm down.

"Ooohhh, hello, Mario."

"Is everything all right? You sound upset."

Not wanting to reveal her encounter with Brogan, she answered, "No, I'm okay. I was outside and ran in when I heard the phone. I was praying it was you."

"Ah! Then your prayer has been answered."

Mario was sitting in a comfortable chair in the living room of his Hancock Park home. The room was now immaculate. Suzanne, wearing panties and a sheer robe, looked drained from cocaine abuse. She sat on the sofa smoking a cigarette and snorted her fourth line in the last hour, then longingly smiled at Mario as he spoke into his cell phone.

"Monday is your day off, si?" he asked.

"Yes…uhm, si," she innocently answered.

"Then let us go shopping…for the party."

There was silence.

Suddenly, Mario eyed the ash on Suzanne's cigarette. He snapped his fingers and angrily pointed to the ashtray next to her. It pissed her off. She didn't like being 'snapped at,' then she reluctantly flicked the ash into it.

Getting back to the call, he said, "Please, cara mia…allow me. It would be my pleasure to dress you."

Sitting on her bed, Jessica felt guilty for accepting his offer.

"But please, Mario, nothing expensive. You've already been too good to me."

"Not to worry. I am looking forward to it. I would be honored."

Jessica cheered up a bit.

"Okay. I'll…I'll see you Monday. Is noon okay?"

"Si," came through the phone, causing her to smile. "Until Monday. Ciao, bella."

A gut instinct made her hesitate before uncomfortably replying, "Ciao."

She hung up, but something about his "Ciao, bella" caused her to look at the phone.

Mario hung up his cell and watched Suzanne snort another line. When he spoke to her, his Italian accent was gone.

"When are you going to stop doing that shit?"

She ignored the question, ground out the cigarette in the ashtray, then stood and walked over to him. Her breasts swayed as she approached. He looked at them under the sheer robe. Knowing he was admiring them, she sensuously squeezed her nipples and cooed, "Like 'em, don'tcha?" Mario grinned. She asked, "How soon before we put our little Madam to work?"

"Let's see how she handles the party. Now come here, my little puttana, and gimme those."

Suzanne giggled as she reached the chair, then straddled his lap and asked, "You always call me that. What's it mean?"

Mario laughed as Suzanne put her breasts in his face.

Positioning her lips to his ear, she whispered, "I love you, Mario."

He didn't respond. His mouth was busy licking and sucking Suzanne's nipples.

CHAPTER 24
Great Ass. Now Turn Around

It was close to one o'clock on Monday afternoon by the time Mario and Jessica stepped into The Lomax Art Gallery.

Patricia sat behind the front desk. An assistant was showing customers several paintings. There were a few others milling about admiring artwork throughout the gallery.

It only took Patricia a second to see the couple, causing her to rise and approach them.

"Hi, Patricia!" Jessica said as they hugged and kissed each other on the cheek, then she looked at Mario and said, "Mario, this is Patricia." She again turned to the artist and said, "And *this* is Mario."

Patricia and Mario shook hands as he put his accent to work, "Jessica has told me much about you. It is a pleasure to meet you."

Patricia responded, "Thank you. And it's a pleasure to meet *you*. I understand you were at my showing."

He scanned the art on the walls and said, "I heard about your paintings and was intrigued." Then he romantically looked at Jessica and continued, "And though your creations are wonderful, I believe I left with the most beautiful work of art that evening."

Jessica swooned as Patricia provocatively replied, "Then I think I have just the painting for you." She led them to a stunning five-foot-high by four-foot-wide painting based on the sketch the artist was working on the day the two women were arrested.

It detailed a woman wearing a majestic blue evening gown covered in sequins, and an exposed red bustier with garters and stockings...but now had Jessica's face.

Jessica was stunned. Mario admired it.

"Remember the sketch, Jess?"

"Oh…my…god," was all Jessica could get out.

"*Magnifica!*" Mario loudly exclaimed.

"I never thought it would end up like *this!*" Jessica declared.

Mario, to the surprise of the women, said "I will take it."

Jessica, astounded, turned to him and asked, "Excuse me?"

He turned to Patricia and proudly said, "I want to make a present of it for my Jessica…and I want you to paint a new one for *me*. Can you do that?"

Without hesitation Patricia answered, "I would *love* to."

"Grazie. Perhaps you would also do me *this* favor? Would you accompany my Jessica on a…how-you-say? A…shopping expedition? A shopping *spree?* We are attending a party this weekend and she would like to find something special to wear." Then Mario pointed to the painting and said, "Perhaps you can also find something for the new portrait, si?"

The women looked at one another. They were grinning like kids.

Mario reached into his pants pocket, pulled out a thick roll of hundreds and handed it to Jessica. "Is twenty-five hundred enough?"

She was speechless.

Patricia put her arm around Jessica and told Mario, "It'll be my pleasure. She's in great hands."

Jessica could not take her eyes off Mario. Her heart was pounding…and she could feel it.

The ladies' first stop was to Agent Provocateur, the classy-yet-naughty lingerie store on Rodeo Drive in Beverly Hills. As a smiling Patricia and a nervous Jessica looked in the window, unbeknownst to them, Detective Brogan slowly drove by and watched.

"Look at this stuff! I've never worn *anything* like this. *Ever*," Jessica confessed. "*Now* I know why Leon said I was boring."

"Welcome to the real world, honey," her friend giggled.

Once they were in the store, Jessica awkwardly watched Patricia riffle through bustiers, garters, stockings and high heels. Jessica shook her head in disbelief that she was actually there.

A short time later, Jessica stepped through the dressing room curtain. Standing before Patricia and the saleswoman, she elegantly modeled an exquisite, blue satin bustier with gold trim, garters and stockings. The ensemble sensuously exposed her breasts and legs, all accentuated by a pair of gold high heels.

Though nervous, Jessica looked tantalizing.

Patricia voiced her opinion, "Great ass. Now turn around." Jessica did as she was told, then her friend said, "I can definitely work with that."

The saleswoman nodded and chimed in with, "So could *I*."

"This is not me," Jessica playfully chuckled. "Why is he making me do this? And why am I *agreeing to it?*"

Patricia answered seriously, "Remember what I said about enjoying the good times? Well, this is one of them. Now take those off." She looked at the saleswoman and commanded, "Wrap them up," then returned her attention to Jessica and said, "Now let's go find you a dress for that party. I know just the place."

CHAPTER 25
I Was Living In One Just A Little Larger

The party that took place on Saturday night, August 5th, brought Jessica back to Brentwood, where Valentina's was once located.

It was a little after nine o'clock as Mario's Mercedes maneuvered through the dark, suburban streets of affluent estates before finally making its way to the very secluded end of North Bundy Drive.

He pulled up to the front gate, provided the security guard his name, then was ushered onto the fourteen-acre property. The Mercedes drove into a large, paved area and parked among the other twenty-plus expensive vehicles.

Exiting the car, Mario and Jessica stood next to one another in the dark and held hands. He could feel her apprehension and nervousness.

An attractive female servant with a lantern approached from a pathway. She wore a long red tuxedo jacket over a black bustier, garters, stockings and heels, and shined the light on Mario's Italian suit and face, then onto Jessica to reveal a long, stylish blue dress that covered one of her shoulders and hugged her body. Gracing her neck was a beautiful necklace that she found while on her "shopping expedition." She was also wearing make-up and had her hair styled, a combination that accentuated her beauty.

"Good evening, Mr. Vissani. Nice to see you again," said the servant.

Mario nodded. Jessica was impressed.

"And what would you like to drink this evening?" the servant asked.

"Due' Rémy Martin, grazie," Mario quickly answered with an Italian flair.

"Merci," came the French reply.

Jessica, still holding Mario's hand, nodded to the servant who then bowed, raised a cell phone and sent a text. She then shined the lantern on the ground and led the couple to the candle-lit walkway that wound through the trees.

Along the way they passed a large, windowless, five car garage that was solidly constructed of brick at the edge of the parking lot. It held Mario's attention.

A couple of minutes later Jessica caught sight of a mansion that looked more like a castle. The servant led them to the front entrance and its two tremendous, ornate wooden doors.

On cue, the doors were opened from inside by a female servant in a French maid's outfit holding a silver tray with two snifters. She professionally greeted Mario and Jessica, bowed, presented their drinks and welcomed the couple inside.

When the doors closed behind them, Jessica, still holding Mario's hand, stood in awe of the opulence. They lingered in the foyer sipping their cognacs as Jessica took it all in. A moment later, a woman in her mid-50s, attractive, very well-dressed and with an Eastern European accent, approached them.

"*Ah, Mario!* So nice to see you," the woman loudly announced. Then she looked at his companion. "And *you* must be Jessica. Finally we meet." She turned to Mario. "She's beautiful, Mario… *beautiful.*"

Jessica was embarrassed, but knew to say, "Thank you. You're very kind."

Mario introduced the well-wisher.

"Jessica, this wonderful flatterer is Kalina, our hostess…and a dear friend."

Kalina and Mario kissed on each cheek, then Kalina extended her hand to Jessica.

As the two women shook hands, Jessica said, "Hello, Kalina. It's very nice to meet you, and…" She looked around. "Thank you for inviting us to your…*castle*."

With a bit of a chuckle, Kalina asked, "Is this your first time to a residence of such size, my dear?"

Jessica couldn't hold back her sarcasm or laughter as she answered lightheartedly, "No. Before I met Mario, I was living in one just a little larger."

Mario laughed and winked at his date.

"She's *darling*, Mario. You must tell me…where did you meet?"

"In an art gallery," Jessica replied.

"Investing in art these days, Mario?" Not waiting for a reply, Kalina changed the subject and said, "Let us go outside so Jessica can meet the others, yes?"

The couple nodded.

Kalina escorted them into the living room where soft music played through speakers and set the appropriate atmosphere. Walking into the huge room, Jessica's attention went directly to the silent, red Steinway baby grand against the far wall. It brought back memories of her Baldwin, which stirred up sadness and longing, and for the next few minutes she found it hard not to think about it.

They passed through the living room doors onto the massive back patio that ran the length of the castle and sported several tables, numerous chairs and chaise lounges.

Kalina led the couple to a table of seven women and five men in their late 20s to mid-60s, all well-dressed and of mixed races. Each had a drink, and a few shared a joint.

Another servant, also in a red bustier, garter and stockings, approached the table with a tray of hors d'oeuvres.

Kalina announced the new arrivals, "I believe you all know Mario, yes?" Everyone smiled, nodded and tipped their glasses. "And this is the simply-wonderful Jessica." Jessica graciously smiled. "It's her first time to my home…so let's make her feel welcome and comfortable," then she signaled the servant. "Bring fresh drinks for us out to *the clearing*." The servant nodded, and with the tray in her hands she obediently returned to the house. Then Kalina turned to Jessica and said, "Come, dear. Let us walk."

A grin was on Jessica's face as Kalina took her arm and led them onto a candle-lit path that headed away from the castle into a copse of trees and manicured hedges. Mario contently strolled a few paces behind.

Jessica looked back as Kalina pulled her along. Mario gave a reassuring smile to let her know the hostess enjoyed giving "the tour."

"How long have you lived here, Kalina?" Jessica asked.

Kalina's free hand waved about as she spoke.

"I've been here for..." She turned her head to look at Mario. "What has it been, darling?"

"I believe...eleven years," he replied.

Kalina smiled at Jessica.

"Eleven years, and they have been very, very wonderful to me. And I have so many friends...some that come by two or three nights a week, and others I don't see for a year or two."

"That must be exhausting, I can see why you have all the servants," Jessica innocently and inoffensively replied, causing Mario and Kalina to chuckle. Jessica, taking a sip of cognac, didn't understand what she said that made them laugh.

"That reminds me, Kalina," Mario interjected as they continued to walk. "I wanted to discuss something with you."

"Yes, darling?"

"I hear you may be looking to sell. Is it true?" he asked as he finished his cognac.

Kalina stopped to face him and asked, "Are you interested?"

"I could be. Let us talk more...later."

"You're thinking of selling this beautiful home?" Jessica asked in astonishment as they strolled.

A break in the hedges led to the pool and hot tub area where soft music could be heard wafting through the balmy night air. On the far edge of the pool, a naked man and woman in their 40s amorously kissed and caressed. Jessica was paying attention to Kalina and hadn't seen them...yet.

"Yes. I'm going back to Europe...to my country where I can live quite comfortably on my savings."

Jessica replied, "I'm glad I got to see it before--"

She cut herself off in mid-sentence, having spied the couple. Mario was amused by his date's stunned reaction. She tried not to show it...but it was evident by the blush in her cheeks.

Noticing they were no longer alone, the couple, unfazed, stopped kissing and smiled at everyone.

Kalina said, "Ah, Mario...of course you remember the Sullivans," then addressed the naked couple, "And this is Jessica." The Sullivans waved. Jessica, still stunned, timidly waved back.

The trio continued along the path as Kalina said, "They're a lovely couple. 'Solar' money."

They walked for another moment before coming upon the clearing.

It was exactly that, a manicured area illuminated by lights and surrounded by trees with music emanating from hidden speakers. In the middle was a table with two well-dressed couples, one in their thirties and the other nearing sixty. Each was enjoying a flute of champagne and the women were sharing a joint.

Mario took Jessica's hand and followed Kalina to the table where the guests were engaged in light conversation. A servant approached from the opposite end of the clearing, placed a bottle of champagne and two snifters of Rémy Martin on the table, briefly and quietly consulted with Kalina, then departed.

Kalina turned to the couple and said, "Unfortunately, I must return to the house to welcome more guests. Would you please introduce yourselves?"

Mario assured her they would, then Kalina stepped away.

Jessica, her necklace now uncentered, watched Kalina disappear along the path until Mario broke her concentration by handing her a fresh snifter of cognac. Taking it, they clinked glasses before they drank.

Mario was about to say something, but his eyes dropped to her neck and chest. Without asking, he reached and straightened the necklace, then said to the others at the table, "My name is Mario, and this is Jessica."

Meanwhile, in the living room of Mario's Hancock Park home Suzanne was smoking a cigarette, had downed a few shots of tequila and snorted a couple of lines as she stared at the clock. She looked like shit…wired…strung out.

She yelled, "*Where are you?*" at the phone. "He's mine, you convict bitch! You *fucking slut!*" Then she flung the shot glass at the clock and missed by a mile.

Mario and Jessica held hands and sipped their drinks as they walked the hedge-lined path with Steve and Dana, the younger couple from the clearing. The sounds of a female's sexual, erotic moans could be heard.

Jessica raised her head to listen. The others were unaffected. Mario eyed Jessica's reaction while the moans grew louder as they continued walking. On a bench lit by candles were two women in their 50s, expensive clothes askew, their hands running through beautiful hair, their lips searched each other's body.

Jessica stopped short.

Mario, Steve and Dana respectfully smiled, briefly watched, then moved along. Mario gently pulled Jessica's hand and she followed.

"We come up this way to visit Kalina and for the golf," Dana nonchalantly said.

"Do you play golf, Mario?" Steve asked.

"Not as well as you, I am sure," Mario cleverly replied.

The path led them back to the pool and hot tub area as the Sullivans were now having sex in a corner of the pool.

Jessica, confused, looked at a calm Mario. Steve and Dana eyed the Sullivans…then looked at one another.

"I'd like to take a dip, hon," Dana said to her husband, then asked Jessica, "How about you?"

Jessica didn't know what to say and turned to Mario as Dana slipped out of her dress and Steve began unbuttoning his shirt.

Mario diplomatically said, "Thank you, but we are going to the house for another drink."

Within seconds, Dana and Steve were naked and stepping into the pool.

Mario tugged on Jessica's hand as she watched the couple.

The path Mario chose took them alongside the large garage where Jessica stopped and leaned against the brick wall.

In the dark, she didn't see Mario eye the structure with more than a little interest as she asked, "Mario…what kind of party is this?"

His attention quickly returned to her.

"Ah, amore mio, sometimes Kalina's friends get…amorous," then he looked deep into her eyes and asked, "Are you uncomfortable?"

"Well, yes. I've never been to anything like this before, but…" She ran her hands through his hair, sensuously kissed him and purred, "I want to be with *you*."

He pulled her closer and they kissed.

She melted as they ravaged each other under the night sky and against the brick wall.

It was midnight when a bustier-clad servant delivered six fluffy robes to the pool area.

Mario, Jessica, Steve, Dana and the Sullivans sat in the hot tub, each in a sexual afterglow.

Everyone smiled at Kalina as she approached.

"Mario…may we speak for a moment?"

He looked at Jessica and asked, "Will you excuse me, cara mia?"

Jessica adoringly smiled and nodded.

As Mario stepped from the hot tub, Dana eyed the tattoo of a red fox on the side of his left shin. She turned to Jessica and remarked, "That's an interesting tattoo."

Jessica, with a still-satisfied grin, again nodded.

Mario put on a robe and followed Kalina to a table on the far side of the pool where they sat and talked.

The others continued to fondle and kiss their partners. Jessica, now relaxed and comfortable with her new friends and the goings on around her, put her head back and looked at the stars. A woman's hand reached and sensuously cupped Jessica's left breast. She didn't react...except to enjoy it.

About an hour later Mario's Mercedes was parked at the curb outside Jessica's North Hollywood apartment...a far cry from the neighborhood and residence they had just come from.

Jessica's lips separated from Mario's as they stood at her door. Their faces were lit by a streetlight. He looked at her content smile and said, "Cara mia, I was hoping that soon...you will come with me to Italy. Is this something you would like?"

For at least the fourth time that night Jessica was *more* than surprised.

Italy...the one place she had always wanted to go.

"It would be a dream come true, Mario."

With a grin on his face, he asked, "Would you like to know what Kalina wanted to talk about?"

"I'm sure it had something to do with selling the castle."

Mario raised an impressed eyebrow.

"Very wise. So? Should I buy it?"

"What would you do with a huge place like that?" Jessica asked.

"I have no idea," he laughed. "But right now...that is not your concern. You must get to sleep. You are sitting for your portrait tomorrow."

They kissed.

She unlocked the door and lovingly said, "Good night, Mario."

"Ciao, bella," he stated, then turned and walked to his car.

As she watched the Mercedes drive away, her expression changed.

It was nearly two in the morning when Mario arrived home to find Suzanne on the sofa smoking a cigarette. There was an open bottle of tequila and a shot glass on the coffee-table, and an ashtray full of butts. She was scanning through TV channels with no sound and looked terrible from the combination of crying, crashing and being wasted.

The sight of her and the room, along with the stale odor, disgusted Mario.

She looked at him.

The Italian accent was no more as he shouted, "Look at this fuckin' place!"

Pissed off, Suzanne responded by yelling, "You were with *her*, weren't you?"

"You *knew* I was." Then rage entered Mario's voice. "You know what's wrong with you? You use too much of that shit. You're so fucked up you can't even sing anymore! You know that's why your band fired you. Just remember…the *only thing* you have going for you *is* Jessica."

"Then why don't you have *her* come over and clean, you psycho-fuck? You're with her so much, why don't you have *her* take care of you? Let *her* fuck you like I do!"

"Shut your mouth," he barked back.

"And what do you mean, she's the *only thing I have going for me?*"

"You know the deal. Now shut up."

"A piece of the action! I get my piece of the castle! You promised! You said once a month I'll get my envelope."

Mario eyed her with disdain, and retorted, "As long as you don't blow it. 'Cause if you do…if she finds out about you and me…I'll have your fuckin' throat cut and dump you in the ocean."

Suzanne was now speechless and afraid. She knew he would do it.

Seeing that she got the point, Mario's attitude changed to cool and slick.

"Tonight I planted the seed. In a couple of months our plan will be making money. A *lot* of money." He briefly turned happy and declared, "And I'll have a place for my equipment." Then he raised an eyebrow, grinned and said, "Now, my little puttana, clean up this mess, take a shower, make yourself fuckable…and come to bed."

As he walked upstairs to the bedroom…she hung her head in despair and did as she was told.

CHAPTER 26
Why Do You Want *Me* In Your Life?

Jessica worked from ten o'clock to three o'clock at the diner, then went home to shower. Afterward, she packed some make-up and hair products, her new bustier, garter, stockings and heels, then boarded an Uber, which Mario had arranged and paid for, and was at The Lomax Art Gallery by six o'clock.

Patricia was with two customers, but excused herself long enough to ask Jessica, "Ready to sit for your portrait?" Jessica happily nodded. "Go into the studio. The make-up and dressing tables are all ready for you. Get yourself together, then call me from your cell and I'll be right there."

And that was exactly what Jessica did.

It took about forty minutes before the subject felt she was ready to be immortalized on canvas, and as promised, Patricia showed up within two minutes of being called.

The women spent a while finding the right pose. Patricia adjusted the lighting and her subject's limbs. When the light and shadow played well together, which added mystery and detail, she proceeded to snap a series of photos.

"I thought you were going to paint me, or at least start etching something on a canvas," Jessica inquired.

"That was in the old days, Jess," Patricia answered. "I take photographs from every angle to get the right details and colors. I'll use the photos as a reference, *then* I'll etch you in this pose. That's when I'll define the contours of your face. When I'm happy with that, I'll put a canvas on the easel and start painting. I'd say it'll be ready in two weeks. Is that okay?"

Jessica was flustered.

"Sure...that's fine. I thought I was going to have to sit here for *hours*. Besides, I still have no idea where I'm going to put the *other one* that Mario bought me."

After the photo session, Patricia loaded them onto a laptop and reviewed them on a 32-inch monitor, then returned Jessica to the pose and began sketching onto an 18x24-inch pad.

The whole session took less than two hours.

Patricia's assistant locked the gallery and left at eight o'clock. An hour later the friends departed through the rear door, got into Patricia's 1962 baby blue Ford Thunderbird convertible and went to Don Cuco in Simi Valley...the planned destination of their celebratory dinner two years earlier.

By the second round of margaritas in the dimly lit booth, the two women were sitting closer to each other than when they arrived...and shared hugs more than once during their laughter and conversations.

When Patricia pulled the Thunderbird to the curb of Jessica's North Hollywood apartment, she raised the convertible top. In the quiet darkness, the two women embraced and kissed. Eventually stepping out and making her way to the apartment's door, Jessica was somewhat surprised at how free and open she was by allowing herself to be kissed and touched by a woman...and felt nothing wrong with it.

She looked back at Patricia and blew a kiss. Patricia smiled, put the car in gear and drove away.

A few days later, on Jessica's day off, she and Mario took a drive up the Pacific Coast Highway to the Leo Carrillo State Park, located at the north end of Malibu.

They spread a large blanket onto the sand and set up an ice bucket, filled it with ice and a bottle of Dom Pérignon with two glass flutes resting next to it. The couple wore bathing suits and relaxed under an umbrella for shade.

Facing one another on the blanket, Jessica looked into his eyes. "Why *me*, Mario? Why do you want *me* in your life?"

With his Italian accent in full swing, he replied, "Because, cara mia, inside and out you are beautiful…and you make me very happy. Have you never had someone love you simply for you? Not for what you have or what you could offer?"

She thought for several seconds, then, still staring into his eyes, she said, "I thought I did. But he left."

With conviction in his voice, Mario responded, "I will not leave, Jessica. I believe I am falling in love with you."

He closed his eyes and kissed her.

Parked along the highway's curb, Detective Brogan sat in an unmarked sedan watching Mario and Jessica through binoculars.

The lovers' lips parted.

"So, tell me, you were to hear from the employment agency, si?" Mario asked.

Jessica shook her head and, very frustrated, said, "Same as the others. The conviction and that damn '*Madam*' label are going to follow me 'til I die." She put on a pair of sunglasses and laid down.

Mario looked toward the ocean as his hand unintentionally came to rest in the sand. He raised it, angrily looked at the grains stuck to it and brushed them off.

Jessica rhetorically said, "It's as if I was being forced back into that business. I mean, if they're going to accuse me of doing something I didn't do, and not let me make an honest living…I may as well do what they *said* I did."

A smile unseen by Jessica appeared on Mario's face as he picked the last individual grains of sand off his hand.

"Maybe you can use The Madam persona to your advantage, cara mia?" he offered.

Jessica turned onto her side and looked at him…inquisitively.

"This is just a thought," he continued, "But, remember when Kalina said she had parties three nights a week, and how, after only eleven years, she was able to retire to Europe?" He slyly raised an eyebrow. "Suppose *I* was to buy the castle and *we* were to have the same type of parties...four or *five* nights a week?" He looked at her. "Kalina will provide us her list of friends, and I am sure there is a clientele, an *elite* clientele, that would love to belong to a private club run by The S-and-M Madam. And there is nothing illegal about it. No massages, no prostitutes...no police. And after a few years, cara mia..." His voice took a loving turn. "You can make enough money to start a new life...the life you want...the life you deserve."

Jessica sat up, lowered her sunglasses, leaned toward the handsome Italian and kissed him.

Brogan watched through the binoculars.

Since Kalina had her parties on Friday, Saturday and Sunday, Mario and Jessica went by to walk through the castle's rooms and grounds early Monday afternoon, August 14th. Jessica took notes as Mario pointed to various walls, windows, walkways and doors. More than once they strolled past the red Steinway. The property, the castle itself and all of its acreage, was picturesque and beautifully appointed, and Jessica liked what she saw.

Kalina walked with the couple along the pathway to the brick garage and opened one of the five doors. It was empty, and Mario liked what *he* saw.

By nightfall, the three of them sat in a Polo Lounge booth at The Beverly Hills Hotel joyfully toasting the sale and kissing each other on the cheek.

The deal was made.

The next day, Jessica tearfully said goodbye to Rosie and the North Hollywood diner.

By the following Tuesday, August 22nd, Mario and Jessica had placed their names on the deed and became the new owners of the castle and its fourteen acres via a wire transfer from Mario's bank in Italy.

Standing in front of the two tremendous ornate wooden doors at sunset...they kissed.

"Thank you for putting me on the deed, Mario...but it was *your* money that made this possible," Jessica said with sincerity.

"It may have been my money, dear Jessica...but it's *you* who they will pay to see and *be seen* with," he told her proudly.

Over the next several days the couple purchased bedroom furniture, a laptop computer to be used for their new business, along with other essentials, and Jessica moved into the massive estate. Mario spent most afternoons and a few nights there, but told her he stayed at the hotel most nights because he needed to prepare documents that were required for early morning meetings with building inspectors, contractors, bank executives and investors for his other properties.

Each evening he made sure to be at the castle to share dinner and a glass of wine on the back patio and to watch the sun go down with his new partner.

During one such evening Mario said, "So in return for Kalina leaving the piano and much of the furniture, you will allow me the garage to store my building equipment, si?"

Jessica smiled as they sealed the deal by tapping their wine glasses.

Suddenly, she had a thought.

"You know, I have a friend, Darryl...he has a limo company. We can contract him to pick up guests. What do you think?"

Mario innocuously replied, "A *very* good idea. Any friend of yours is a paisan of mine."

Once again, they toasted and drank.

It was decided they would have their first party over the upcoming Labor Day weekend, from Friday September 1st to Monday the 4th. Jessica quickly went to work sending invitations via emails to Kalina's distribution list informing them of a four-day bash hosted by the castle's new owner...The S&M Madam.

Reservations and credit card confirmations came in faster than Jessica could log them.

The following Tuesday, August 29th, Jessica drove her newly leased 2016 black Jaguar XK8 convertible to Beverly Hills to personally hand-deliver Patricia's invitation to the upcoming weekend's party.

While Patricia was dealing with customers, Jessica killed time by perusing a few paintings until her friend approached and asked, "Have you found a place for your two portraits yet?"

"*Yes!*" Jessica proudly announced. "We put the first one in the master bedroom and the new one in the living room over the fireplace for *everyone* to see." Then she went into her purse and extended the engraved invitation to the artist. "And this is for you."

Again, the two women embraced and kissed before Jessica departed.

CHAPTER 27
I Have To Get Back What Volpe And Prison Took Away

The next afternoon, and with only two days before their first party, Jessica was working with the servant staff she inherited from Kalina, along with her new head chef, Constance, and the new manager and front door host, Charlie…her friends from Valentina's.

She had contacted them with the news of her good fortune, and after a long, emotional conversation, Jessica was happy to have them in her employ…and they were happy to *be* employed. What took place at the parties wouldn't involve either of them, and they were fine with that.

Mario was overseeing the delivery of his equipment into the large brick garage when Patricia came by to see the paintings, tour the property and hang out with Jessica.

The women eventually made their way into the living room and stood next to the red Steinway, which allowed Patricia the perfect angle to admire her artwork. She was impressed by the way the second painting was hung above the fireplace and the special lighting that was focused on it.

Jessica comfortably sat on the piano bench as it readily became obvious that over the last ten days of living there, she had spent a large amount of time practicing. Her fingers touched the piano's keyboard, gracefully playing arpeggios.

Patricia came up behind Jessica, placed her hands on the pianist's shoulders and began massaging them as Jessica continued to play.

"It's almost unbelievable, Jess. One day you're alone and living in a one room apartment…" The artist looked around the large opulent space. "And the next, you've got a prince and a castle on a hill. It's every girl's dream."

Jessica stopped playing, looked around to see that they were alone…then turned serious.

"*You* started a new life, Patricia…now it's *my* turn. I have to get back what Volpe and prison took away from me."

"Good girl," came from the more streetwise Patricia.

"Remember when you told me I needed to find out what my mission was?" Jessica asked as Patricia nodded, then she confidently continued, "Well, I *found* it…and I'm *on* it.

"And it's…?" Patricia asked.

Jessica just grinned, letting her friend know she didn't want to reveal it, then began playing "*Come Back To Sorrento*," just as she had four nights a week in Valentina's.

Patricia didn't get the significance of the song. That was when she stopped Jessica's hands from playing.

The pianist looked up at her, inquisitively.

The expression on Patricia's face showed genuine concern for her friend's safety and well-being. Jessica could tell Patricia was serious about what was going to be said.

"Whatever that mission *is*, Jess, you'd better have a fail-safe just in case something goes wrong. It's not like you're opening an art gallery. If anything happens again, you need to become invisible… like Volpe did."

Jessica knowingly muttered under her breath, "Yeah…like Volpe did." She began playing *Sorrento* again as she said, "You know, Patricia, a wise man once told me, 'Anger clouds your path to clarity and it pains your heart. You must not hold anger within. You must use it. You must release it, or…it will devour you.'"

Patricia giggled, "Actually, that sounds like something our old friend Mr. Watanabe would say."

Jessica stopped playing, grinned, faked a bad Asian accent and responded, "Ah, you are very wise, Grasshopper."

CHAPTER 28
Welcome To The Castle!

By nine o'clock on Friday night, September 1st, the castle's parking lot was filled with high-end vehicles. One of three tuxedoed servants approached two guests as they emerged from their car. A black stretch limo pulled in and parked. Darryl exited the front door and opened the rear door so that Steve, Dana and the Sullivans could step out and be met by another servant, give their drink order and be led along the path they had walked many times before.

As guests approached the entrance, the front door opened to reveal a red bustier clad woman with their drinks. She then steered them toward Charlie, who stood at a podium in his tuxedo. "Welcome to the castle!" he would greet everyone with a smile, and then checked their names against his list of those who had pre-paid.

More than a dozen guests had made their way into the living room to mix and mingle with old and new friends, and to admire the portrait of their new hostess, which was perfectly positioned above the fireplace.

Beautiful women from twenty-five to sixty wearing erotic bustiers, garters, stockings and high heels, served drinks and hors d'oeuvres.

On the patio, twenty-plus people socialized as servers provided food and libations. Patricia sat on a chair chatting with guests.

In the pool and hot tub area, some guests were naked, and sensuously enjoying each other in various combinations. Others sat poolside, at tables and on chaise lounges drinking, smoking marijuana, smiling and kissing. A servant brought clean towels and robes, knowing more guests would be there and would need them.

The first floor of the castle consisted of the huge living room, a TV room that ran erotic films, a long dining room table used as a buffet for Constance's array of gourmet finger food, the kitchen, which was off limits to guests, and three full bathrooms.

The second floor contained ten bedrooms and six full bathrooms for guests to enjoy themselves in. A staff of five saw to it that each room was cleaned, the sheets and towels were constantly replaced and were always ready for the next revelers of hedonistic pleasures.

The third floor, accessed via stairs and an elevator that went to all floors, was Jessica's and Mario's living quarters and was off limits to guests and employees.

In the stylishly decorated third floor office, Mario and Darryl sat across the desk from each other. Mario was wearing a custom-tailored suit and silk tie. Darryl wore a basic 'off-the-rack' suit and tie.

The impressed limo driver leaned toward Mario and said, "*You did it*. You got her to front the place…and you got big-money out there payin' to hang with 'The Madam.'"

Mario grinned proudly, but said nothing as he fiddled with a pair of binoculars he kept atop the desk.

Darryl changed the subject and softly said, "Here's the deposit from your friends for their next order." Then he picked up a briefcase that was next to him, put it on the desk, turned it toward Mario and opened it. It was stacked with bundles of $100 bills. They looked at one another and nodded. Mario set the binoculars in their specific location on the desk, removed two bundles of cash and placed the case on the floor. He threw one bundle to Darryl who caught it…but didn't know why.

Without his accent, Mario said, "This is the last time I'm telling you. Burn what you're wearing and go see my tailor. If you want a bigger part in this operation, *my* operation, you need to look like you know what you're doing. Got it?"

Darryl obediently nodded and put the cash in his pocket. Mario opened the top drawer, took a keyring holding a large and a small key and used the small one to unlock a side drawer where he put the other bundle of cash next to a .38 revolver. He shut and locked the drawer, then returned the keys from where they came.

Mario opened the office door to make sure no one was around, then the two men boarded the elevator and went to the first floor.

As Darryl returned to his limo in the parking lot, Mario walked into the living room to see several people surrounding the Steinway as Jessica flawlessly played "*This Masquerade*" for them. He approached and looked at Jessica…admiring her.

Just after two in the morning, Mario and Jessica waved to the last four guests as they departed along the path to their cars, then the two partners held each other in the moonlight and kissed.

In his thick Italian accent, Mario said, "Your first night was a fantastic success, my love…my cara mia! Brava!"

Jessica couldn't be happier, until he said, "But I must leave, too. Another meeting with the building inspectors in the morning and all of the paperwork I need is at my home and the hotel."

"When will you be back?" she asked in her usual manner.

"Tomorrow afternoon before everything starts…I promise."

They held each other and kissed again before Mario walked to his Mercedes parked next to Jessica's Jaguar in the circular driveway in front of the castle.

Blowing a kiss in her direction, he said, "Ciao, bella," then drove away.

CHAPTER 29
La Volpe Nella Foresta

It was Monday, November 20th, 2017, only three days before Thanksgiving and another gala weekend party at the castle. It had been an amazingly profitable few months since the Labor Day opening, and Jessica and Mario couldn't have been happier.

Having lunch with Patricia every Monday had become the norm for the two women, so it was no surprise when Jessica arrived at The Lomax Art Gallery at one o'clock.

While Patricia was finishing a new piece in the studio and an assistant was catering to some customers, Jessica killed time by perusing a few paintings, then stopped to look at a book on the front desk titled, "*The Art Of Italia*," and flipped through its pages.

Suddenly, something caught her eye.

It was the photo of a painting that depicted a red fox meandering among trees. Below the picture was the title, "*La Volpe Nella Foresta - The Fox Of The Forest.*"

Jessica stared at the title and image for a few seconds, then shut the book as Patricia approached and asked, "Ready?"

The question brought Jessica back to the moment. She changed her look of intense concentration to one of happiness as she told her friend, "Yes, and I'm starving!"

Happy for their time together and chatting along the way, Jessica and Patricia strolled leisurely to one of the nearby Beverly Hills bistros.

As soon as Jessica returned to the castle, she went directly to the master bedroom, opened her purse, removed her wallet, rummaged through several business cards, found Brogan's, took out her cell phone...and dialed.

Mario rarely stayed over on Monday evenings, so, being alone in the castle, Jessica played it safe and waited until midnight before she did some investigating.

Walking down the hall from the master suite, Jessica, dressed in jeans, a T-shirt and sneakers, entered the office, turned on the light, sat at Mario's desk and opened the top drawer. Inside it was as orderly as a desk drawer could be. It contained legal pads with business notes about his properties, the castle's accounting ledger filled with their business's expenses, assets and the names of their membership, plus a neat line-up of pens and paperclips. There was nothing out of the ordinary...other than the keyring holding the two keys.

She opened the other desk drawers, but found only one of them locked. She took a shot and slipped in the small key, turned it to the right and unlocked it. Sliding the drawer open, her eyes widened at the sight of the .38 revolver resting on top of twelve stacks of $100 bills, each with a wrapper showing "$10,000."

She immediately shut the drawer, locked it, then put the keys in her pocket, walked to the doorway, turned off the light and went to the elevator.

It was very dark outside as the moon was in a waxing crescent phase. Jessica knew it was best not to turn on the pathway lights, so she brought a flashlight to find her way to the brick garage. Using the large key to unlock the center door, she entered and turned the flashlight toward the interior. Three-quarters of the space was filled with six-foot-long crates bearing French printing on them. She walked among them until coming upon an open crate, then moved the cover and looked inside.

Grasping the gravity of what she saw, Jessica returned the crate's cover to its original position, and with conviction in her eyes she locked the door and returned to the castle to place the keys in the office desk.

She made a phone call, left a message…then went to bed.

At 4:47 the next afternoon, Jessica's Jaguar was parked at a scenic overlook along Mulholland Drive. She stood along the wooden railing at the hilltop's viewpoint…watching the sun begin to touch the horizon.

Detective Brogan parked his car and, limping, approached Jessica from behind. Without turning, she knew he was there.

He softly said, "Beautiful, isn't it?"

She didn't move. She let the sun bathe her face for a few more seconds…then looked at him. He recognized immediately that she appeared more confident than the last time they were face-to-face outside of her one-room North Hollywood apartment.

He got right to business.

"It's happening tomorrow morning, and you've got to make sure he's there. Can you do that?"

"Yes, and *I* want to be there. I want him to know it was…me."

Not taking his eyes from her, he said what he always wanted to tell her.

"You know, in my gut, I always knew you were innocent…but there wasn't anything I could do about it. I've felt terrible about it since it happened. You have no idea how many days and nights I worked on that case, even *after* it was closed. The dead bodies connected to Volpe's business, but no way to tie him in. The--"

Jessica interrupted, "Dead bodies?"

"That woman Pamela Sorel, the one you replaced, and the German therapist named Ingrid. Remember them?"

"Yeah."

"Both of 'em had their throats cut and dumped in the ocean a month apart down in Mexico. Over the last four years, six girls disappeared from their jobs at high class massage parlors Volpe used as fronts for his 'business'…and not one law enforcement agency had a thing on him."

"Fuck," slipped out of her in shocked amazement.

"Not one of the databases showed *anything* about a *Volpe*. You gotta believe me, Jessica, I never stopped looking."

She affectionately gazed at him…appreciating his honesty, then emphatically said, "Now we'll *both* be closing that chapter." Next, she asked the detective a question he didn't see coming. "Have you ever…have you ever felt alone? Empty?"

He saw her pain. It was a tender and honest moment they were sharing, so he waited a few seconds before answering.

"One afternoon six years ago, my wife wanted to go to some music store…something for her piano. So we took the drive. It was the wrong time to go shopping." He turned his head from Jessica's eyes and looked at the sun's final rays dipping behind the San Gabriel Mountains as twilight graced the valley below, then continued. "There was a gun deal going down in the parking lot. Things must've gone bad. Everyone started shooting. Fucking machine guns. Strays went all over the place." He closed his eyes as he recounted, "One of 'em hit my wife," then he again looked at Jessica, tapped his left leg and kept going. "Two hit me. I shot three of 'em before I was hit and went down. The rest of 'em took off." He teared up and said, "My wife died." He took a deep sigh, recovered and went on. "So yeah…you could say I know the feeling of being alone and empty." He shook his head and closed with, "We *both* deserve more than what life's handed us, Jessica."

She stared into his eyes.

He went to caress her face…but stopped. He remembered that he was a cop.

Jessica broke the silence.

"I'm not going to lose this time, Tom. I didn't look back…and I'll *never* look back again."

He was unsure of what she meant, but he had other information he had to tell her and got right to it.

"You know, after tomorrow, life may be even tougher for you. They're gonna close down the castle. You'll be homeless again…and you gotta be careful. This guy's no small-time punk. He's smart, dangerous and he kills people."

"And he's sly. Just like…a fox," she added with a bit of sarcasm.

The sun's light was gone.

"I don't know what I can do, Jessica, but somehow…I'm going to make this up to you."

Jessica chuckled as she told him, "You know, I made someone in prison a promise like that. The sad part is, I don't know if I'll ever be able to keep it."

Then she kissed Brogan on the cheek and walked to her Jaguar.

CHAPTER 30
And Don't Bleed On My Carpet, Puttana

It was 5:42PM by the time Jessica drove her Jaguar into the illuminated circular driveway and parked next to Mario's Mercedes.

Normally, every Wednesday through Sunday night, the castle would be bustling with ten servants, two bartenders and the kitchen crew as they prepared for another night of "members." But, seeing as it was Tuesday, all was quiet when she entered.

Typically, Mario would greet her at the front door, but not today. Jessica assumed he was in the garage dealing with his "equipment," so she made her way to the elevator and took it to the third floor.

She walked toward the master suite, but noticed the office light was on and the door was ajar. She walked to the door, quietly opened it and watched as Mario, with his back to her, was slipping a briefcase and duffle bag into a large 5-foot tall safe...a safe that had not been there earlier that day.

He closed and locked the steel door, then stood and turned to see Jessica eyeing the safe. He was startled and stuttered in order to apply his Italian accent.

He was able to get out, "*Madone*, Jessica! What the hell are you doing sneaking up on me like that?"

She pointed to the safe and asked, "What the fuck is *that?*"

Having to think fast, he came up with, "I...uh, I thought it would be good to have one here. I had a few of the workers from my house bring it over."

"Why? What's in there?"

"Paperwork for my buildings, some cash I use for the building inspectors and my workers, plus the books for the business, credit card records and documents for *this* house."

She just glared at him.

There was only one way out of it. He walked toward her… mixing 'slick' with romance, and said, "Now that the renovations at my home have finally been completed…I sold it. In a few days *this* will be where I will live, my cara mia. To be here…with you."

He ran his hands through her hair and put his arms around her. As they kissed, he pressed her against the wall while grinding his body into hers. Not wanting him to suspect her hate and rage, Jessica responded with feigned fervor. Her hands pulled his hair, ripped his shirt, then visibly and viciously dug into and clawed his back.

It had turned into a marathon sex session.

By nine o'clock, both were drained.

After a late dinner, Jessica, wearing a T-shirt and shorts, sat in bed looking over the accounting ledger and inputting the figures into the laptop computer next to her. Patricia's first painting faced the bed from the far side of the room that Jessica, its subject, would often look at with fondness.

Mario, having just come out of the shower, walked past her wearing a towel around his waist. Jessica noticed the deep scratches she had made on his back and shoulders as he proceeded to their walk-in closet to dress.

Jessica, who was deeply involved in the ledger, raised her head to look at him as he emerged from the closet.

"Where you going, sweetheart?" she asked, knowing, as per Brogan, that Mario needed to be at the castle the following morning.

"I have to get more contracts from my place for a meeting. But I will be back later. In a few hours."

She seductively cooed, "Can we have breakfast tomorrow... here? Just you and me?"

"There is nothing I would love to do more, my Jessica," he answered as he kissed her, then sat on a chair to put on his shoes.

She held up the ledger that also contained their business's "membership list," and said, "This is one hell of a bottom line, Mario. Who wouldn't love a two-hundred-and-twelve percent profit after four weeks? You're a genius!"

"I told you, if we do this right, this castle is our mine-of-gold," he replied using his fake broken-English as he stood, put on a sport jacket and began to leave. Then he stopped at the doorway, blew her a kiss and smoothly said, "Ciao, bella."

And he was gone.

She now hated those words.

Jessica hopped out of bed, walked to the window, waited, then watched Mario's Mercedes slowly move down the driveway. But instead of heading to the street, the car turned toward the parking area...and out of sight. She ran to the office for a better view. Not turning on the lights, she grabbed the binoculars from the desk, went to the window that faced the parking area and watched as Mario parked, exited and walked toward the front of his car, then stood in between the headlights.

There was another car in the dark waiting for him. She watched the driver step out, open the backdoor, take out three large duffel bags, then close the doors.

Feet ensconced in a new pair of shoes walked on the asphalt parking lot. Darryl, in a handsome new suit, appeared in the beams of the Mercedes' lights and dropped the duffle bags.

Mario walked toward him, shook the black man's hand and, sans accent, said, "Lookin' good. Lookin' *very* good."

"Thank your tailor, dog," came the reply.

Jessica was still watching through the binoculars and became enraged at seeing Darryl once he appeared in the light.

Mario walked to the bags, then he bent over and unzipped them. They were full of bundled $100 bills.

"Is it all here?" Mario asked.

Darryl said with a grin, "Three million on the nose. One million in each bag."

Mario simply gave a nod, then stood as Darryl loaded the bags into the Mercedes' trunk, then got in his Cadillac and drove away.

Jessica stepped away from the window and replaced the binoculars to their exact location. Then she thought about Darryl, the one person she had praised and defended for helping her after being released from prison.

Vengeance was in her eyes.

It was nearly eleven o'clock by the time the Mercedes pulled into Mario's Hancock Park driveway. He noticed the living room light was on.

Upon entering, he found Suzanne smoking a cigarette, dressed elegantly, but wired on coke and sitting on the sofa watching TV.

Smiling at her appearance and without any accent, he said, "Hi, Suzanne. You look very nice."

She turned the TV off, stood and *snapped* at him.

"Were you with *her* again? You said you were gonna be back three fucking hours ago. You said you were finally taking *me* out!"

He wasn't going to tell her he was late because he had to fuck 'The Madam,' so he stalled as he stepped over to the bar, poured himself a scotch, then slyly smiled and said, "There was a problem. I had to take care of it...or she would've caught on."

"You fucked her!" Suzanne yelled. "That's what you had to take care of, isn't it?"

He took an envelope from his jacket and tossed it to her.

"That should keep you happy 'til next month."

She angrily threw the envelope on the floor.

"You said you were gonna be home *early!*" she continued to yell. "I got dressed! We were going out! I'm fuckin' *starving!* I've been sitting here for--"

Out of nowhere, Mario yelled louder.

"Hey, stupid! She almost caught me taking care of business. I had to stay with her for a while. What did you *expect* me to do? Let her in on everything? Then I'd have to cut you *out!* You want that? At least *she's* not busting my balls all the time."

"What are you gonna do? Have Darryl kill me like he killed Pammie?" Suzanne hissed with fire in her eyes. Enraged, she picked up the ashtray and flung it at him. It missed by a foot and smashed into the wall.

Mario assessed the damage and the mess, turned irate, then rushed to her, grabbed her throat and slapped her face...hard, causing her to fall to the floor. He barked, "You know, I used to *like* having you around. You were fun. You looked good. You even *fucked* good." He picked up the envelope, put it in his pocket, went to the bar, then looked at her and continued, "But you kept snorting that shit. Day-in, day-out. That's all you fucking do. *Now* look at you."

She stared up at him. Her nose and lip were bleeding.

In a most disgusted voice, he growled, "Go clean yourself up... and don't bleed on my carpet, puttana." Then he pointed to the ashtray and ordered, "Then clean up this mess."

He downed the rest of the scotch, turned and left the house.

As he shut the door behind him, Suzanne screamed, "*You fucking bastard!*" then wiped the blood from her face...and smeared it on the carpet.

She angrily took a full vial of coke from her purse, put it to her nose and inhaled...hard.

Mario's car headed in the direction of Brentwood as he tapped a programmed button on his cell phone.

Darryl was driving south on Sunset Blvd when his phone rang. He looked at the Caller ID, then answered it via the car's Bluetooth and said, "I thought you were in for the night."

"Get the truck and meet me at the castle. In the street. Quick," Mario commanded.

"Problem?"

"The coke-head. She's acting up again," came from the disgusted Mario. "I want the garage empty. I don't know what she's capable of. We'll keep everything in the truck until we take care of her. After that, everything will go back to normal."

Darryl understood what that meant. He said, "See you in an hour," then disconnected the call and accelerated.

CHAPTER 31
Not Tonight, Motherfucker

Parked on the street outside the gate to the castle sat Darryl in the cab of a 26-foot box truck with its engine off…waiting.

Within minutes, Mario's car pulled alongside. He turned off the lights, lowered his window and said, "We have to do this without waking up the princess. Wait here. I'll get the key for the garage and put the duffle bags in the safe. I'll call once I do that, then meet me at the garage. Drive in…but no lights." Then he turned sinister as he ordered, "If Suzanne shows up, get rid of her."

The normally peaceful Darryl radiated evil as he gave a slight nod.

The gate electronically opened. Mario pulled his car in and, with his lights off, slowly drove toward the castle and parked behind Jessica's Jaguar. He looked up at the master bedroom windows and was happy to see they were dark.

He struggled to climb the three flights of stairs with the duffle bags to ensure the sound of the elevator didn't wake Jessica. In near darkness, Mario quietly walked past the open master suite door toward the office.

A few minutes later and inside the dimly lit room, he stood in front of the safe looking at its contents of a briefcase and the four duffle bags, each filled with one-million dollars in $10,000 bundles of $100 bills.

Darryl stood outside the entrance waiting for Mario's call when a BMW convertible recklessly drove up and screeched to a stop.

The door flew open and Suzanne, still elegantly dressed, but with a bloodied, bruised and swollen face, bolted out…wired and yelling.

"Where is he, Darryl? In *there?* With *her?*"

Darryl quickly approached Suzanne with a smile and tried to calm her down.

"Hey, Suzie, Suzie, Suzie. Take it easy, baby. He's just making a pit stop to get something for *you*." Then he put both hands on her shoulders. "He'll be out in five minutes, but first…" He rubbed his nose and continued, "C'mere. I got something. The *special* stuff."

Suddenly, with his body close to hers, Suzanne's arm went back for momentum, then forward…hard…and then up. There was a tearing sound.

Darryl doubled over and dropped to his knees groaning in pain. Suzanne was holding a large kitchen knife that was now covered in Darryl's blood. She grabbed his hair and raised his head so he could see her, then said, "So? You gonna throw *me* in the ocean, too? Not tonight, motherfucker." Then she slashed his throat.

He gurgled as blood gushed onto her hand and dress. His body keeled over…dead. She struggled to drag him onto the curb next to the truck, then removed a 9mm semi-automatic from his hip-holster, got in her car, turned off the lights, drove through the open gate and pulled into the driveway.

Mario, with the safe door still open and the keyring in his hand, took out his cell phone and tapped a button.

The sound of a ringing phone could be heard coming from Darryl's dead body.

Frustrated, Mario ended the call just as the room lights were turned on.

He froze and looked up to see Jessica in the doorway…angry.

In his nervousness he almost forgot to use his Italian accent.

"Jesus Christ, Jessica. What are you trying to do? Give me a fucking heart attack?"

She walked over to the desk, looked at the duffel bags in the safe and asked, "What's going on, Mario?" He was speechless. "What's in the bags?" she pressed.

He regained his composure.

"This? Money. Money for the damn building inspector. I did not mean to wake you, cara mia. I am so sorry."

"You didn't wake me...and that looks like a hell of a lot of cash to bribe a building inspector."

She raised her hand revealing the .38 revolver he had stashed in the drawer. With her finger on the trigger, she pointed it at him, and with vengeance in her voice, she said, "The game's over... *Volpe.*"

Rage filled his eyes. He became furious...insane...and lost the accent as he barked, "Why couldn't you just accept what I said and enjoy your life?"

Jessica's hand fretfully shook as she held the gun and said, "The accent...you lying fucking bastard."

"What is it with you fuckin' bitches? Why can't you ever leave well-enough alone?"

"Because she's *innocent*, asshole!" came from Suzanne standing in the doorway. Mario and Jessica turned to see her. Each were shocked...but for different reasons. The wired woman was holding Darryl's 9mm in her bloody hand and it was pointed right at Mario. "She was *always* innocent...until you and me fucked up her life."

"*Suzanne?*" Jessica yelled.

Mario simply uttered, "Fuck!"

Suzanne sarcastically said, "Hello, Jess. Miss me?"

"*What are you doing here?*" Jessica asked in total confusion, then noticed the blood on Suzanne's dress and hands. "What happened to you?"

Looking at Jessica, Suzanne replied, "The blood? I'm okay. It's his delivery-boy Darryl's blood." Then she turned to Mario and laughed, "And don't worry, Mario, I'll try not to get any on the carpet." She returned her focus to Jessica and explained,

"Sweetheart, me and this cocksucker's been playin' you since the day you got out of prison. Shit, even before you *went* to prison. Once we heard you were getting out--"

"*We?*" Jessica interrupted.

"Yeah, '*we*.' I told him…if we had the S-and-M Madam fronting this place, we could make a fortune and--"

"*Shut the fuck up!*" Mario yelled.

But Suzanne continued.

"And finance his *real* business. That's who this bastard is, Jess! A piece-of-shit gun dealer…and you played right into the plan. And if the castle got busted, he was gonna disappear and let you take the fall *again*."

"I said *shut up*, puttana!" he again yelled.

This time it was Suzanne who turned up the volume.

"And I wanna know *what that means, motherfucker!*"

"Just get out of here," Mario commanded. "I'll take care of her and see you back at the house."

Jessica was frantic and confused as she asked, "*What* house? What are you talking about?"

Suzanne had only one thing on her mind.

"I wanna know what…puttana…*means!*"

Jessica yelled back, "Jesus, Suzanne! Puttana…it's Italian for '*slut!*' A '*whore!*' Everybody knows that! Even *I* know that! Now, what the--"

Enraged, Suzanne stared at Mario and said, "*Slut?* You've been calling me a *slut?* Your little fucking *whore?*"

"I said *shut the fuck up!*" he bellowed.

Stunned, Jessica dropped her guard and slightly lowered the gun as she asked Mario, "You *know* her? You've been *sleeping* with her? You two were *in on this?*"

"Oh, honey," Suzanne replied. "He's been fucking both of us good…*real* good. Didn't you, Volpe?"

Suzanne cocked the gun's hammer and aimed at Mario's heart.

Mario moved quickly. He dropped the keyring to the floor, grabbed Jessica's hand with the gun, slapped her to the side and pulled the revolver from her fingers. Jessica slammed into the safe.

Suzanne aimed for Mario and fired.

BAM!

The bullet hit the wall, narrowly missing Jessica.

He quickly turned, cocked the revolver's hammer and pulled the trigger.

BAM!

Suzanne took a bullet to her stomach. With the gun still in her hand, she went flying back and down to the floor.

"*Nooooooo!*" Jessica screamed.

Mario then pointed the gun toward Jessica. Insanity was in his eyes and the Italian accent returned.

"Now, cara mia…I'm afraid I have no alternative but to kill you." He cocked the hammer. "If only you were not so innocent. So naive. So trusting." He again lost the accent. "So…fucking… foolish."

Jessica was ready to die. Her eyes and words burned with vengeance as she let out, "The police know *everything*. I just wish I could be here when they take you away…*Volpe*, you piece of shit!"

With disgust and rage in his eyes, he mockingly snarled, "Ciao…*bella.*"

BAM!

Jessica stood…shocked.

Mario's eyes went wide.

BAM! BAM!

Blood ran from Mario's lips. He dropped the gun, fell to his knees and looked at Jessica…they were both confused.

With three holes in his chest gushing blood, Mario Vissani fell to the floor…dead.

Jessica turned toward the doorway to see Suzanne sitting against the wall bleeding from her stomach and mouth…and holding the smoking 9mm in her raised hand.

Barely able to speak, Suzanne managed a raspy whisper, "Sorry...Jess," then her arm dropped. She was dead.

Jessica was frantic. She looked at Mario's body, then grabbed one of the duffle bags in the safe and unzipped it to find it filled with cash. She quickly pulled out the others and unzipped them to find each contained the same, then popped open the briefcase and scanned files listing names, weapons, prices and dates.

Remembering Andrea Hernandez's actions in the prison's library, Jessica used her shirt to wipe her fingerprints off the briefcase and revolver, then left them next to Mario. Picking up the keyring, she used the small key, opened the cash-filled drawer, removed the fifteen bundles it held and put them in one of the bags. Then she zippered each one and pulled them to the doorway.

Gunsmoke lingered in the air.

Jessica resisted looking at Suzanne's bloodied body against the wall as she struggled to drag the bags out of the room...but she inevitably did.

Leaving them in the hallway, Jessica ran into the bedroom to get her purse, cell phone and car fob, but not before looking at her portrait on the wall. Then she picked up the ledger with its membership list and laptop computer from where she had left them on the bed and slid them into one of the duffle bags.

Outside of the castle, Mario's Mercedes and Suzanne's BMW were parked behind Jessica's Jaguar. She nervously struggled to put the duffle bags in the trunk and back seat of her car, then started it and pulled away.

Anxiously reaching into her purse, she pulled out her phone and tapped a programmed number. It rang twice, then Patricia's voice came through the car's Bluetooth.

Jessica didn't have time for pleasantries as she blurted, "Patricia...I'm sorry. I know it's late. I...I need to come by. Now."

The black Jaguar zoomed out of the driveway, passing the truck and Darryl's body.

CHAPTER 32
I Bet The Sunsets Are Beautiful There, Too

At 6:55AM. just as the sun peeked over the horizon, L.A. County Sheriffs' Deputies, a SWAT team of twelve, plus teams of FBI and ATF agents maneuvered along the castle's driveway and parking lot…making no secret of their arrival, but not before finding Darryl's body outside the gate. It was only a few minutes later when one of them came across the two bodies on the third floor…and the contents of the briefcase.

But the big score was the large, windowless, brick garage.

It only took a second to blow the lock off the door, causing everyone to flood in. A minute later they began filming everything and ripping the crates open with crowbars.

The first ten crates were filled with Uzi's. Others had TEK 9's, followed by AR15's and boxes of ammo for everything from handguns to assault rifles to shotguns to 50mm heavy machine guns. Several were full of one-shot missile launchers and hand grenades, and others were loaded with M-16's.

In every LAX terminal, inside and out, detectives were holding up flyers of Jessica's 'Diamond Jim's mug shot' and scanning the women passing by. Many were stopped and questioned for just a slight resemblance.

At Gate 42 of Alitalia Airlines' boarding area in the International Terminal, people were standing in line to get on Flight 163 to Naples, scheduled to depart at 4:50PM. It was now 4:14PM.

Detective Brogan casually approached, still with his limp, and surveyed the crowd.

A blonde woman wearing a business suit and sunglasses walked toward the boarding area. She looked at the "Now Boarding" sign over the door and smiled.

Brogan saw her as each got closer. Even with the disguise, he knew it was Jessica.

That was when she saw him.

With only a few feet between them, they stopped in their tracks...staring at one another. She was frozen. She couldn't move. He took a deep breath and stepped forward so that they were practically nose-to-nose.

He looked at the flight information above the gate to see she was flying into Naples...then returned his eyes to Jessica and innocently said, "I bet the sunsets are beautiful there, too."

Jessica's eyes didn't stray. Her expression didn't change. She was on a mission and she didn't want it to end now. She took a deep breath...unsure of what the next moment held. It was all in Brogan's hands now.

"Be careful and take care of yourself," he went on to say. "And... and *never* look back."

Motionless, they gazed into each other's eyes, then Brogan stepped aside, knowing he would never see her again.

Jessica, visibly grateful, sighed in relief and walked toward the gate.

As the person in front of her was dealing with the male boarding pass attendant, Jessica reached into her purse and took out an envelope of documents. She removed a small piece of sketchpad paper that read, "Like I once said, you never know when you'll need to be someone else at a moment's notice. Love, Patricia." Jessica fondly smiled, then looked at the wrinkled birth certificate, a new passport and a driver's license...all with the same name, date of birth and vital statistics.

It was Jessica's turn.

She stepped forward and handed her boarding pass and passport to the attendant. He opened it to see the picture of a blonde Jessica…and the name "Francine Ciambrone." He eyed the woman before him. She confidently smiled. He returned the scanned boarding pass and passport, and said, "Grazia, senora." She nodded and walked onto the jetway…not looking back.

From a distance, Brogan smiled, then pulled out the flyer of Jessica's mug shot and limped into the crowd scanning the faces of more women. He was, after all, a cop just doing his job.

A few days later, Charlie and Constance each received a package in the mail with the castle's address in the upper left corner.

Upon opening them, each recipient found a handwritten note that read, "*Shhhh!* Sorry it ended so fast. Love J." Below the note they each discovered five $10,000 stacks.

CHAPTER 33
Did You Look Back?

It was Monday, February 5th, 2018, and a comfortable 74 degrees at the bus station in Madera, California.

Andrea Hernandez, wearing an out-of-style business suit and holding a small suitcase, stepped out of a police car.

She was free.

She looked up to the sky, took a deep breath and rested on the same bench where Jessica sat the day she was released from prison.

A baby blue 1962 Thunderbird convertible with its windows and top down pulled to the curb.

Andrea looked at the car.

"Andrea Hernandez?" Patricia asked from behind the wheel.

The newly released woman suspiciously looked at her.

"Did you look back?" the woman in the car asked.

"Who are *you?*" Andrea cautiously demanded.

"About two years ago you did a favor for a mutual friend…in the library. Let's just say you were roommates. She asked me to give you these."

Patricia held out a stuffed manila envelope and a standard letter envelope with Andrea's name on them.

Intrigued, but still cautious, Andrea approached the car, took the letter envelope, pulled out a sheet of paper and read out loud…

"I told you I'd thank you someday and somehow. Today's the day, and this is how. We all need help when we restart our lives. Love, Jessica." Andrea remembered, smiled and tears filled her eyes.

Then she opened the manila envelope to find it filled with five $10,000 bundles of $100 bills. Overcome with sentiment and gratitude, she openly wept.

"Our friend also told me to offer you a ride. So…anyplace special?" Patricia asked.

Andrea shook her head, slipped the envelopes into her suitcase, stepped toward the car, put the suitcase on the backseat and got in. Patricia extended her hand and they shook.

"Hi, Andrea…Patricia. Like art?"

One afternoon two weeks later, a US postal worker walked into The Lomax Art Gallery and handed a stack of mail to the fashionably dressed and happy Andrea.

Andrea found Patricia in her usual spot behind her office desk and passed along the mail. Looking through the envelopes, the artist waited for her employee to leave before pouring herself a snifter of Rémy Martin and opened an International Mail envelope with a post office box in Sorrento, Italy as its return address. She removed a half-page ad from a local newspaper showing a picture of an attractive black-haired woman who looked remarkably like Jessica named Francine Ciambrone playing piano in a classy Italian restaurant not unlike Valentina's. There was a typed note stapled to the page that read, "Looking forward to your next masterpiece! Love, Francine."

Patricia raised the snifter in a toast to the picture, then sat back, grinned and drank.

CHAPTER 34
Come Back To Sorrento

A delivery truck unhurriedly drove through the Italian countryside.

Pulling up to a comfortable, old villa, he heard a piano playing *Come Back To Sorrento* through its open windows.

Going to the rear of the truck and humming along with the music, the delivery man took out a thin wooden crate, six-foot high by five-foot wide, addressed to Francine Ciambrone and carried it to the front door of the house.

At the sound of the bell, the music stopped and a black-haired Jessica came to the door. The delivery man carried the crate into the living room and gingerly leaned it against the wall next to a Baldwin baby grand.

After locking the door behind him, she laid the crate on the floor and expertly opened it with a crowbar, as if she had performed the task a dozen times before…revealing one of Patricia's framed five-foot by four-foot paintings.

Smiling, Jessica, now 35 years old, poured herself a snifter of Rémy Martin. She removed the picture from the crate, turned it over and laid the front down onto the hardwood floor, then, with a knife, she carefully sliced the protective seal from the back of the frame, revealing hundreds of $100 bills that lined the back of the painting.

She grinned, looked at the walls of her home that were lined with several of Patricia's erotic paintings, then sipped the cognac.

The End

CAST OF CHARACTERS
In Order Of Appearance

Jessica Ross Farber   A talented pianist who was 31 years old at the beginning, and 35 at the end. She just wanted a calm and peaceful life with her husband and piano.

Charlie   The classy manager and maître d' of Valentina's.

Constance   The head chef of Valentina's.

Leon Farber   Jessica's husband.

Sylvia Estrada-Pincus   Guatemalan woman who owned a housecleaning company.

Michael Pincus   Sylvia's husband, 26 years older than her.

Suzanne Ariza   Jessica's friend. Singer in the band Two Ton Sun.

Pamela Sorel   Former receptionist at Diamond Jim's.

Debra "Nurse Debbie" Johnson   A massage therapist at Diamond Jim's.

Darryl Bowling   In charge of Security at Diamond Jim's.

Patricia Lomax/Ketchum/Callahan   A massage therapist at Diamond Jim's, and Jessica's friend.

Ingrid Schüttel   A massage therapist at Diamond Jim's. Originally from Germany (see Bridget Lang).

Peter	A Diamond Jim's client.
Volpe	The unknown owner of Diamond Jim's.
Tia Nash	A massage therapist at Diamond Jim's.
Detective Tom Brogan	Undercover detective in charge of the Diamond Jim's bust.
Mr. Watanabe	A Japanese client of Diamond Jim's.
Lois Hansen	Jessica's divorce attorney.
Nicholas Barker	Jessica's useless court appointed attorney.
Captain Harrell	Detective Brogan's superior.
Nancy Henline	The judge presiding over the Diamond Jim's bust.
Carly Mocco	A massage therapist at Diamond Jim's.
Lisa Barlow	A massage therapist at Diamond Jim's.
Dolores Robbins	A massage therapist at Diamond Jim's.
Karen Knight	The prison bully.
Andrea Hernandez	Jessica's prison cellmate.
Kim Fornicola	A sex partner of Leon Farber.
Bridget Lang	Ingrid Schüttel's real name.
Warden Carpenter	In charge of the Central California Women's Facility.
Rosie	Manager of the North Hollywood diner where Jessica worked.
Mario Vissani	Italian gentleman who swept Jessica off her feet.
Kalina	Owner of "the castle." Mid-50s, attractive and from Eastern Europe.
Steve & Dana	A couple Jessica met at the castle.
Francine Ciambrone	Jessica's new identity.

Made in the USA
Middletown, DE
09 August 2021